MAX STEEL™

•HAYWIRE•

STORY BY
TOM PINCHUK

WHAT IF THE ULTIMATE SUPERPOWER CAME WITH A MIND OF ITS OWN?

To the world at large, turbocharged Max Steel is the newest, coolest, most beloved superhero. To the secret organization of N-Tek, he's their number one ally in the ongoing fight against mayhem, monsters and alien invasion. And to supervillains, he's the only source of Turbo Energy in the universe and therefore incredibly valuable and sought after—by any means necessary. But really, he's just 16-year-old Maxwell McGrath, former regular guy, who's got a whole bunch of crazy new powers and now has to figure out how to live constantly connected (and sometimes merged) to N'Baro AksSteel X377, a wisecracking alien with an attitude who's not always the most cooperative partner. Together, these two friends from different worlds combine to make one superhero...and will have to figure out how to save the universe!

MAX & STEEL

Two heads are better than one, unless one belongs to a stubborn teenager and the other belongs to a headstrong alien. Somehow, these two have to learn to cooperate as one entity, superhero Max Steel!

THE ELEMENTORS

Independently each Elementor is already a tough customer with enough power to knock any superhero for a loop. But together they are almost unstoppable, with more force than a thousand storms.

FIRE

AIR

WATER

EARTH

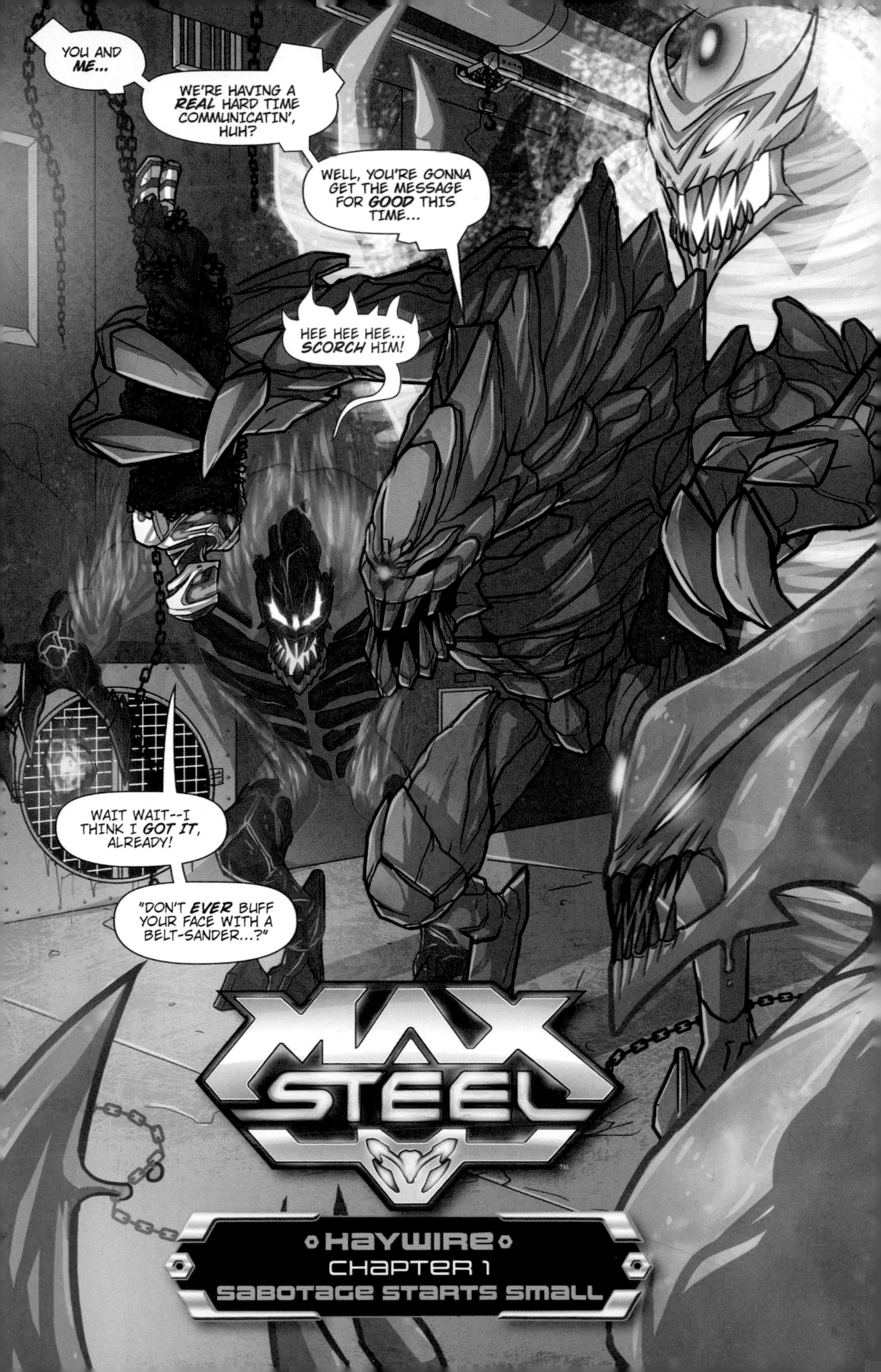
YOU AND ME...
WE'RE HAVING A REAL HARD TIME COMMUNICATIN', HUH?
WELL, YOU'RE GONNA GET THE MESSAGE FOR GOOD THIS TIME...
HEE HEE HEE... SCORCH HIM!
WAIT WAIT--I THINK I GOT IT, ALREADY!
"DON'T EVER BUFF YOUR FACE WITH A BELT-SANDER...?"
MAX STEEL
HAYWIRE
CHAPTER 1
SABOTAGE STARTS SMALL

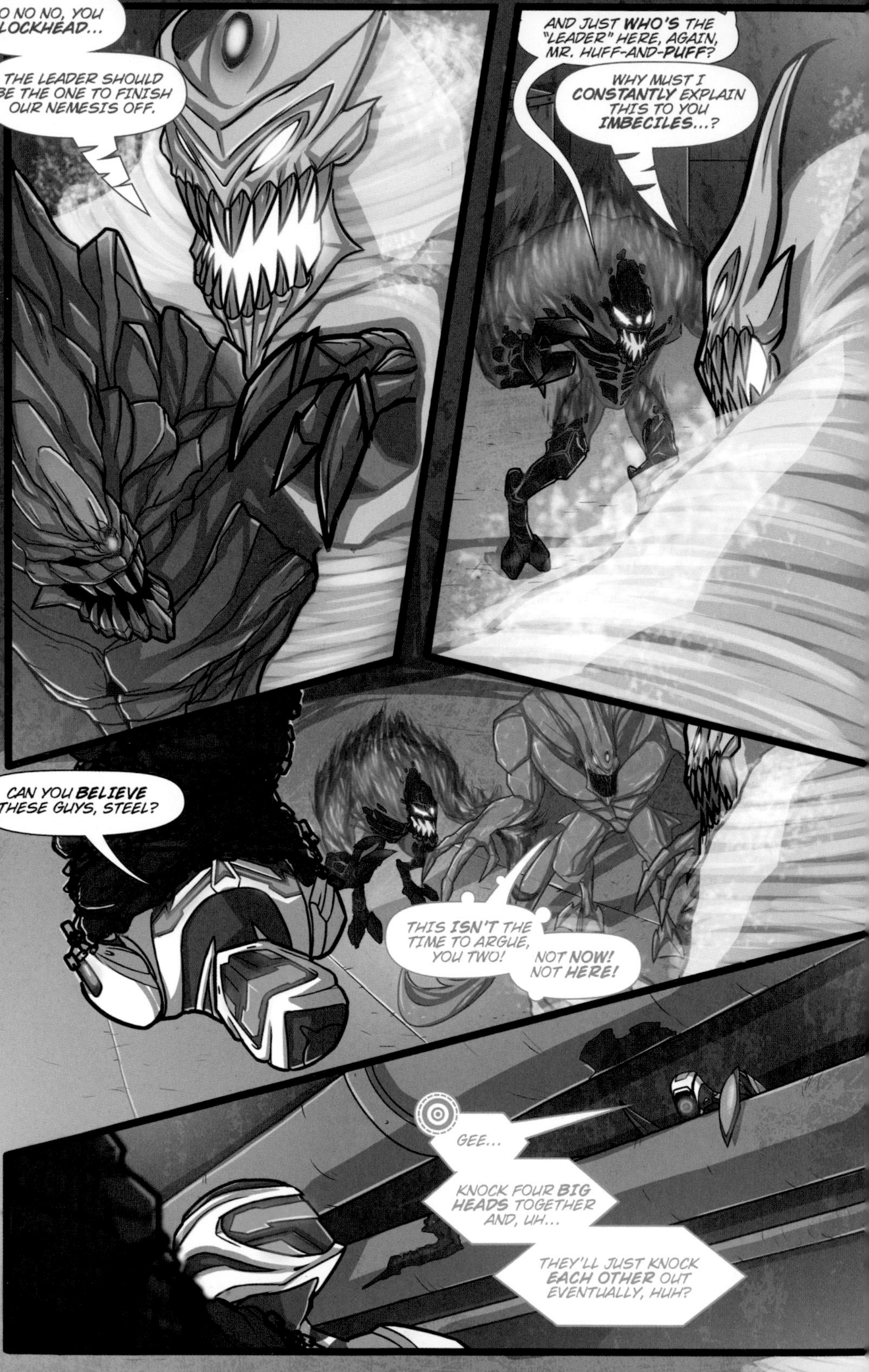
NO NO NO, YOU BLOCKHEAD...
THE LEADER SHOULD BE THE ONE TO FINISH OUR NEMESIS OFF.
AND JUST WHO'S THE "LEADER" HERE, AGAIN, MR. HUFF-AND-PUFF?
WHY MUST I CONSTANTLY EXPLAIN THIS TO YOU IMBECILES...?
CAN YOU BELIEVE THESE GUYS, STEEL?
THIS ISN'T THE TIME TO ARGUE, YOU TWO!
NOT NOW! NOT HERE!
GEE...
KNOCK FOUR BIG HEADS TOGETHER AND, UH...
THEY'LL JUST KNOCK EACH OTHER OUT EVENTUALLY, HUH?

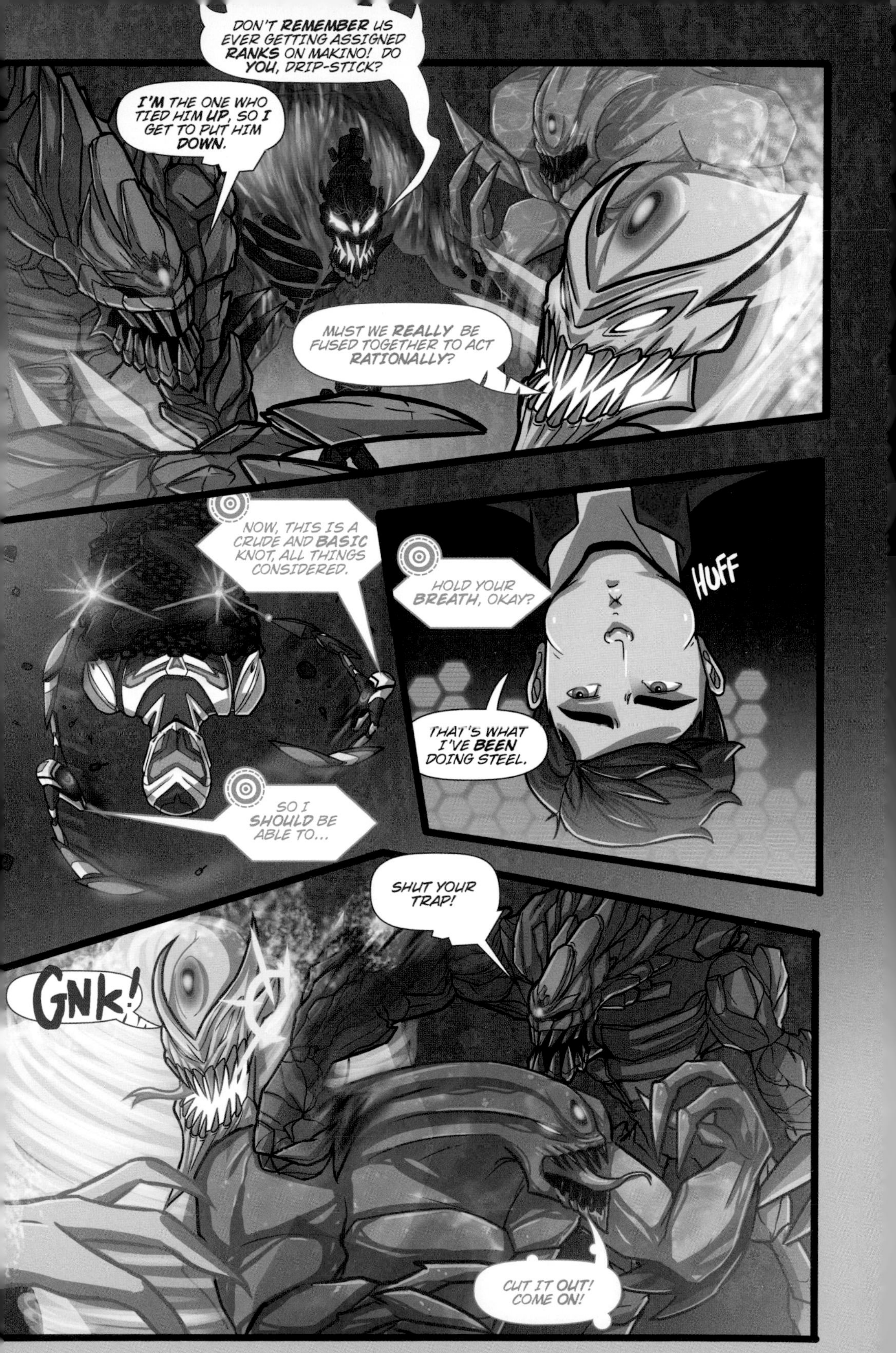

DON'T **REMEMBER** US EVER GETTING ASSIGNED **RANKS** ON MAKINO! DO **YOU**, DRIP-STICK?
I'M THE ONE WHO TIED HIM **UP**, SO **I** GET TO PUT HIM **DOWN**.
MUST WE **REALLY** BE FUSED TOGETHER TO ACT **RATIONALLY**?
NOW, THIS IS A CRUDE AND **BASIC** KNOT, ALL THINGS CONSIDERED.
SO I **SHOULD** BE ABLE TO...
HOLD YOUR **BREATH**, OKAY?
HUFF
THAT'S WHAT I'VE **BEEN** DOING STEEL.
SHUT YOUR TRAP!
GNK!
CUT IT OUT! COME ON!

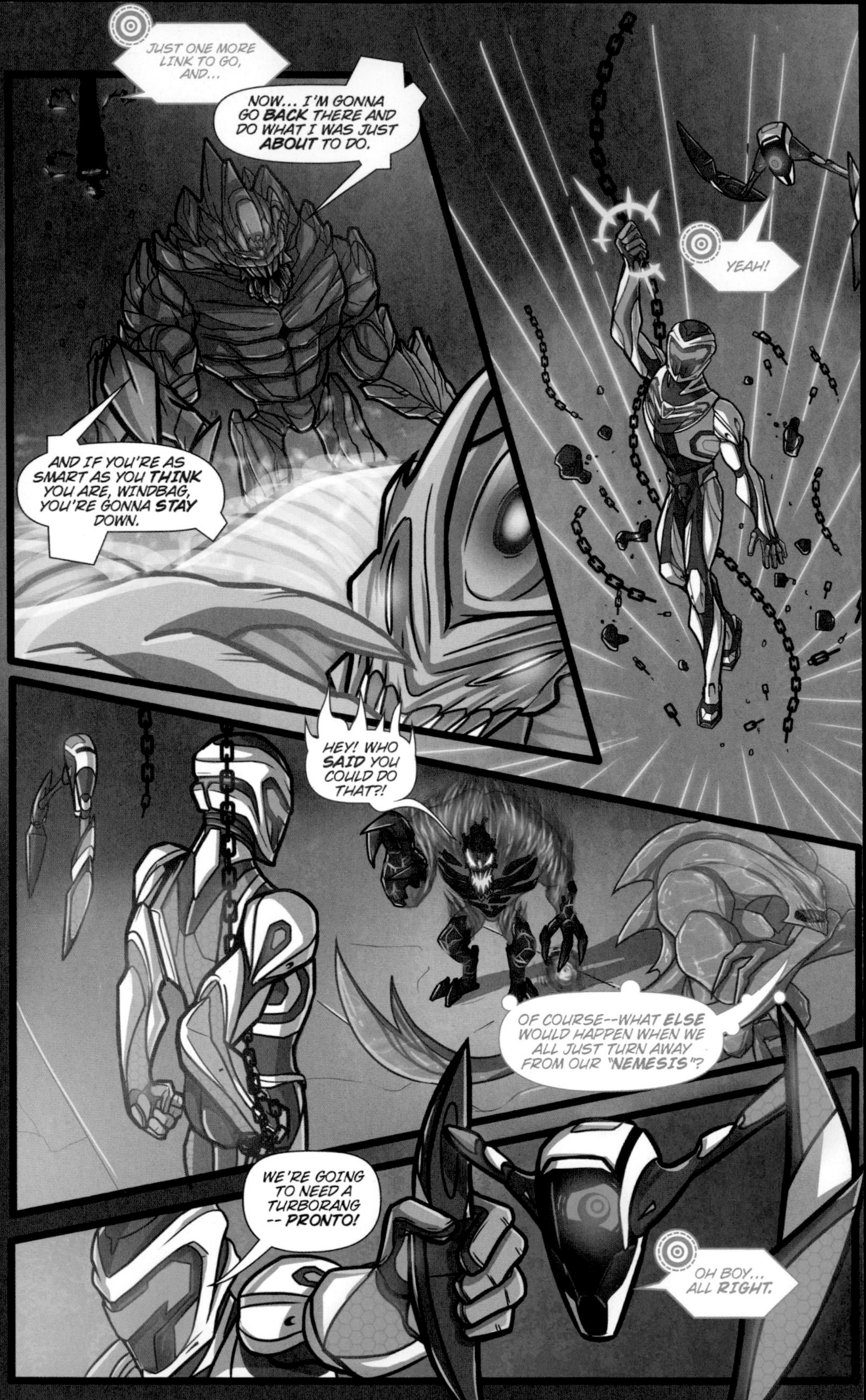
JUST ONE MORE LINK TO GO, AND...
NOW... I'M GONNA GO BACK THERE AND DO WHAT I WAS JUST ABOUT TO DO.
AND IF YOU'RE AS SMART AS YOU THINK YOU ARE, WINDBAG, YOU'RE GONNA STAY DOWN.
YEAH!
HEY! WHO SAID YOU COULD DO THAT?!
OF COURSE--WHAT ELSE WOULD HAPPEN WHEN WE ALL JUST TURN AWAY FROM OUR "NEMESIS"?
WE'RE GOING TO NEED A TURBORANG -- PRONTO!
OH BOY... ALL RIGHT.

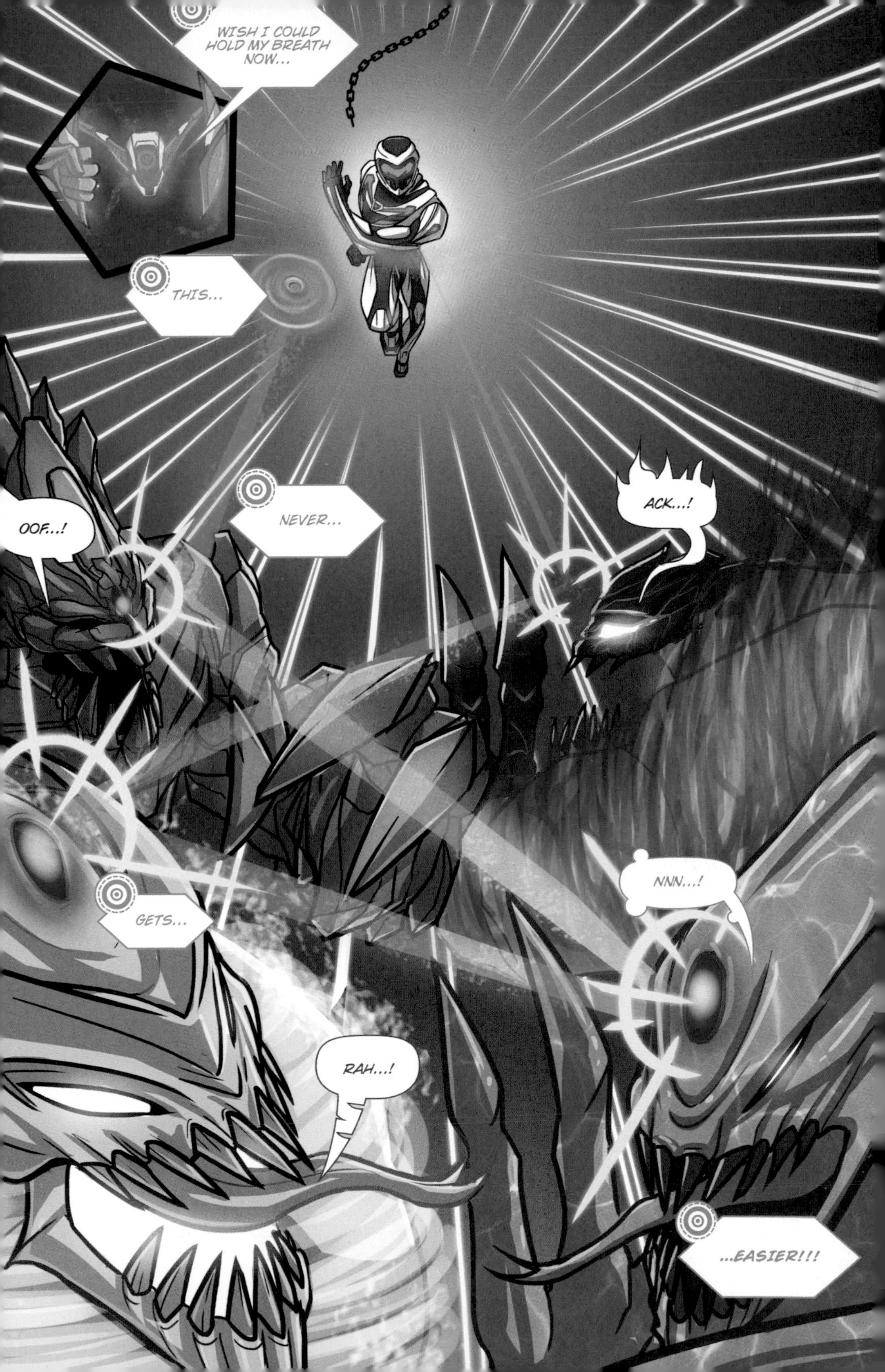
WISH I COULD HOLD MY BREATH NOW...
THIS...
NEVER...
OOF...!
ACK...!
GETS...
NNN...!
RAH...!
...EASIER!!!

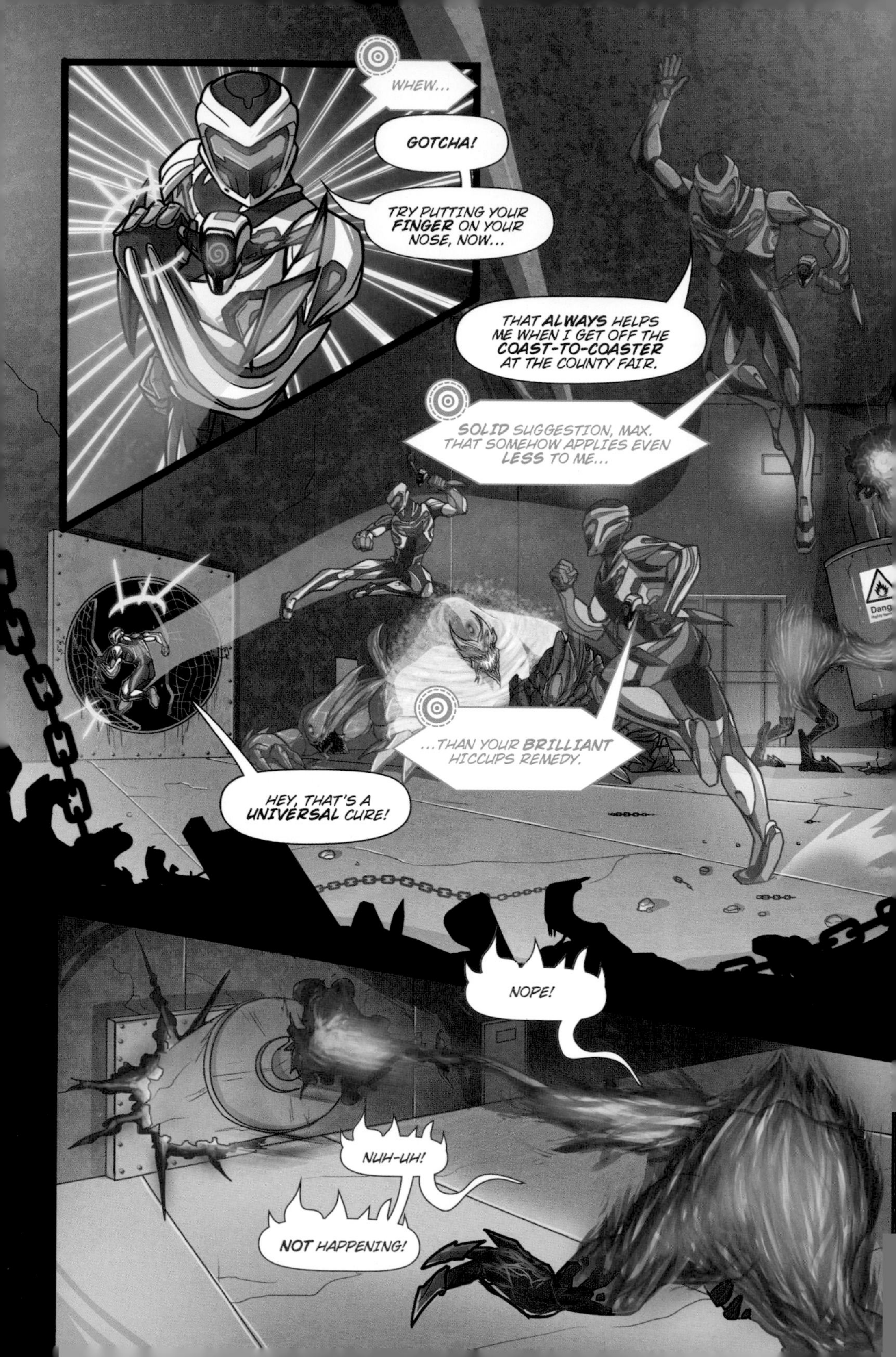
WHEW...
GOTCHA!
TRY PUTTING YOUR FINGER ON YOUR NOSE, NOW...
THAT ALWAYS HELPS ME WHEN I GET OFF THE COAST-TO-COASTER AT THE COUNTY FAIR.
SOLID SUGGESTION, MAX. THAT SOMEHOW APPLIES EVEN LESS TO ME...
...THAN YOUR BRILLIANT HICCUPS REMEDY.
HEY, THAT'S A UNIVERSAL CURE!
NOPE!
NUH-UH!
NOT HAPPENING!

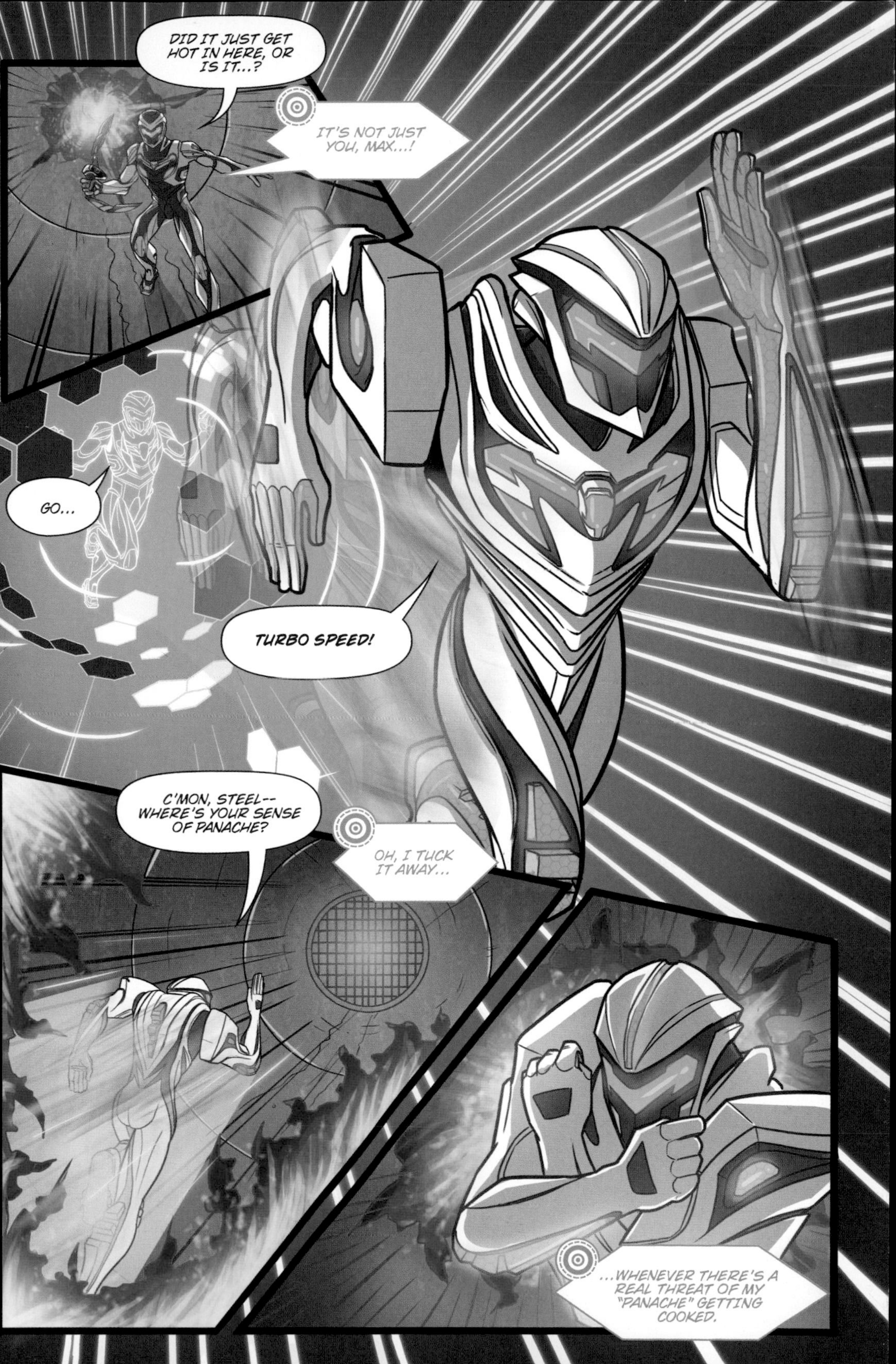
DID IT JUST GET HOT IN HERE, OR IS IT...?
IT'S NOT JUST YOU, MAX...!
GO...
TURBO SPEED!
C'MON, STEEL-- WHERE'S YOUR SENSE OF PANACHE?
OH, I TUCK IT AWAY...
...WHENEVER THERE'S A REAL THREAT OF MY "PANACHE" GETTING COOKED.

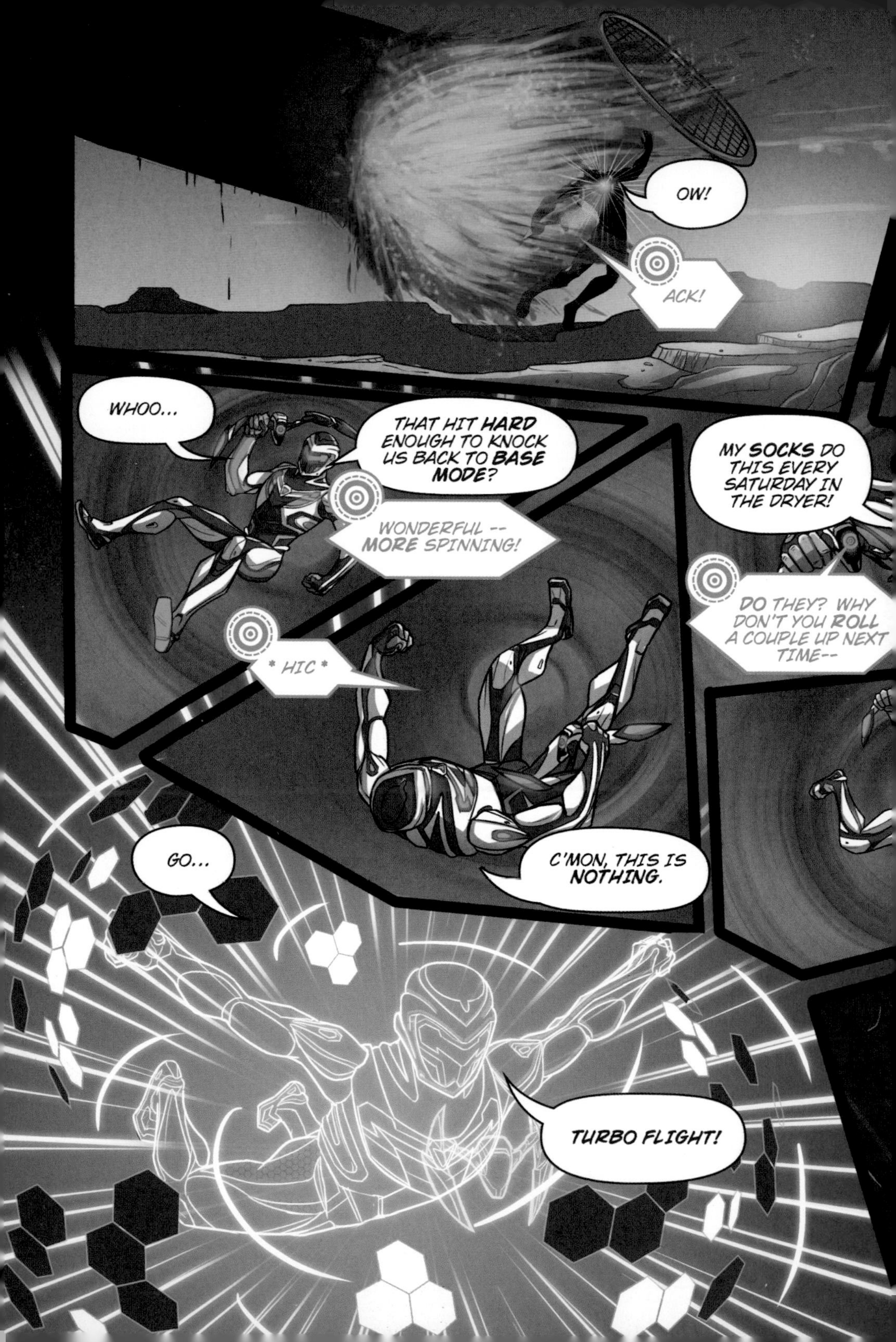
OW!
ACK!
WHOO...
THAT HIT HARD ENOUGH TO KNOCK US BACK TO BASE MODE?
WONDERFUL -- MORE SPINNING!
* HIC *
MY SOCKS DO THIS EVERY SATURDAY IN THE DRYER!
DO THEY? WHY DON'T YOU ROLL A COUPLE UP NEXT TIME--
C'MON, THIS IS NOTHING.
GO...
TURBO FLIGHT!

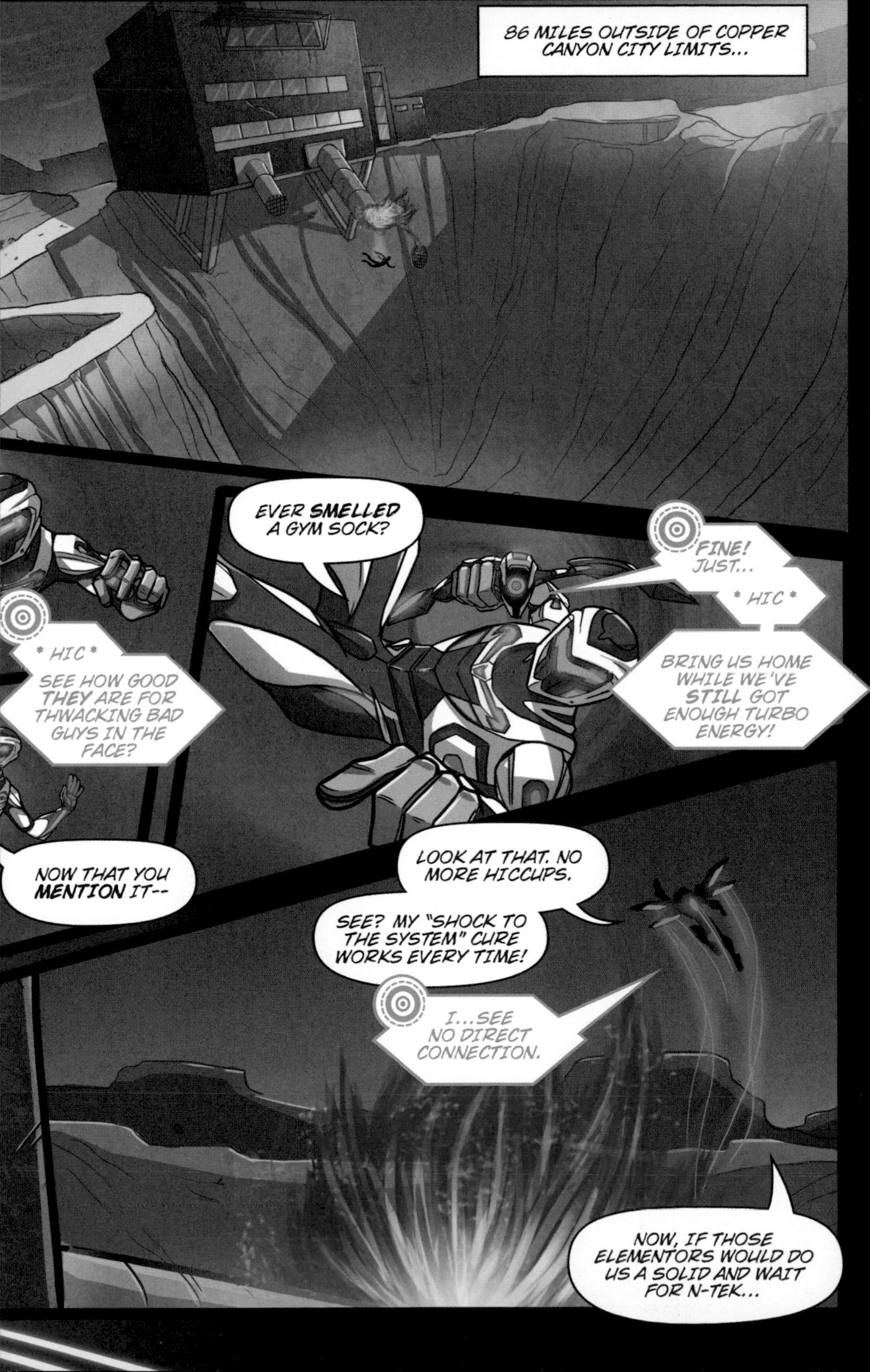

86 MILES OUTSIDE OF COPPER CANYON CITY LIMITS...
EVER SMELLED A GYM SOCK?
* HIC * SEE HOW GOOD THEY ARE FOR THWACKING BAD GUYS IN THE FACE?
FINE! JUST...
* HIC *
BRING US HOME WHILE WE'VE STILL GOT ENOUGH TURBO ENERGY!
NOW THAT YOU MENTION IT--
LOOK AT THAT. NO MORE HICCUPS.
SEE? MY "SHOCK TO THE SYSTEM" CURE WORKS EVERY TIME!
I...SEE NO DIRECT CONNECTION.
NOW, IF THOSE ELEMENTORS WOULD DO US A SOLID AND WAIT FOR N-TEK...

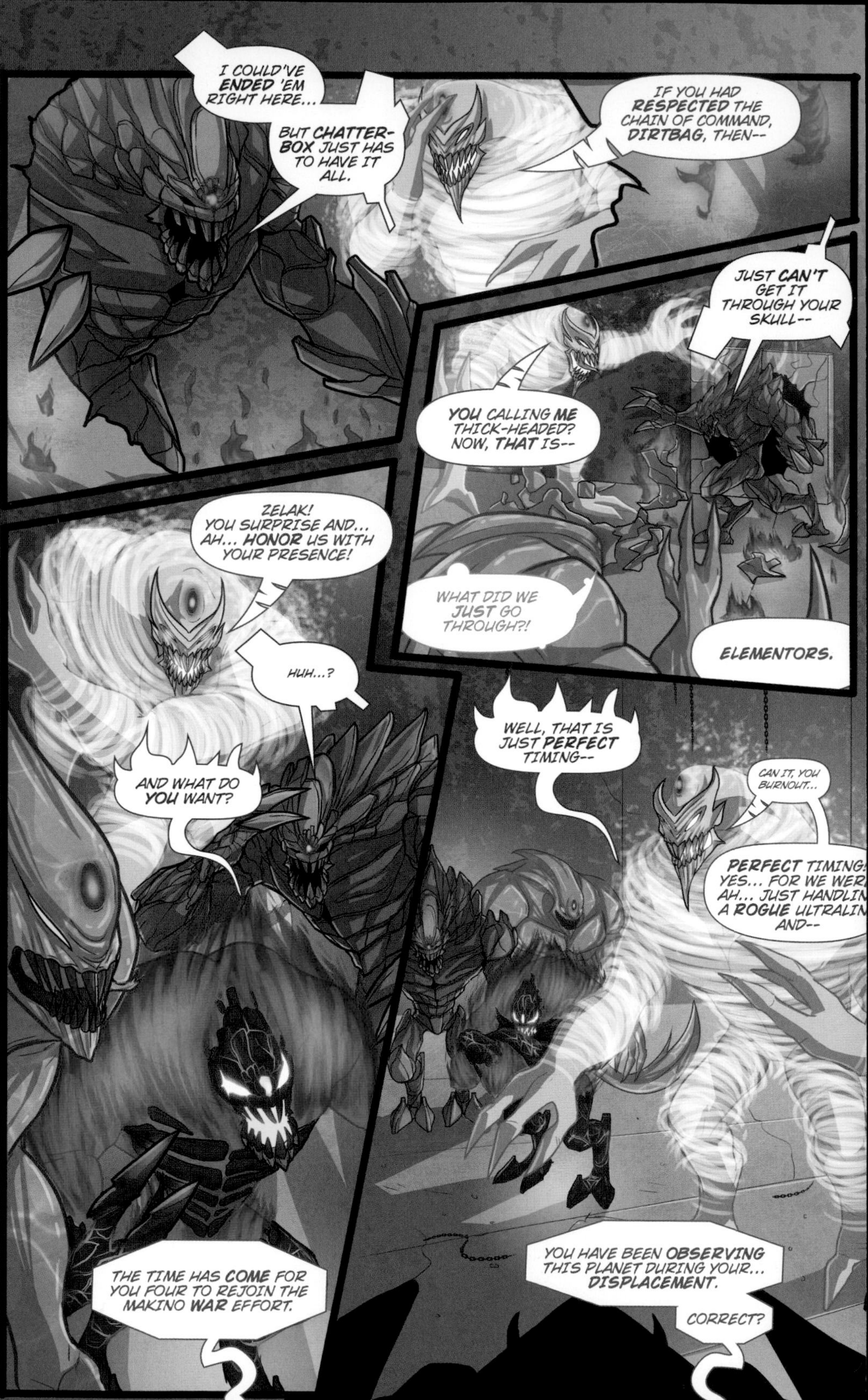

I COULD'VE **ENDED** 'EM RIGHT HERE...
BUT **CHATTER-BOX** JUST HAS TO HAVE IT ALL.
IF YOU HAD **RESPECTED** THE CHAIN OF COMMAND, **DIRTBAG**, THEN--
JUST **CAN'T** GET IT THROUGH YOUR SKULL--
YOU CALLING **ME** THICK-HEADED? NOW, **THAT** IS--
WHAT DID WE **JUST** GO THROUGH?!
ELEMENTORS.
ZELAK! YOU SURPRISE AND... AH... **HONOR** US WITH YOUR PRESENCE!
HUH...?
AND WHAT DO **YOU** WANT?
WELL, THAT IS JUST **PERFECT** TIMING--
CAN IT, YOU BURNOUT...
PERFECT TIMING! YES... FOR WE WER AH... JUST HANDLIN A **ROGUE** ULTRALIN AND--
THE TIME HAS **COME** FOR YOU FOUR TO REJOIN THE MAKINO **WAR** EFFORT.
YOU HAVE BEEN **OBSERVING** THIS PLANET DURING YOUR... **DISPLACEMENT**.
CORRECT?

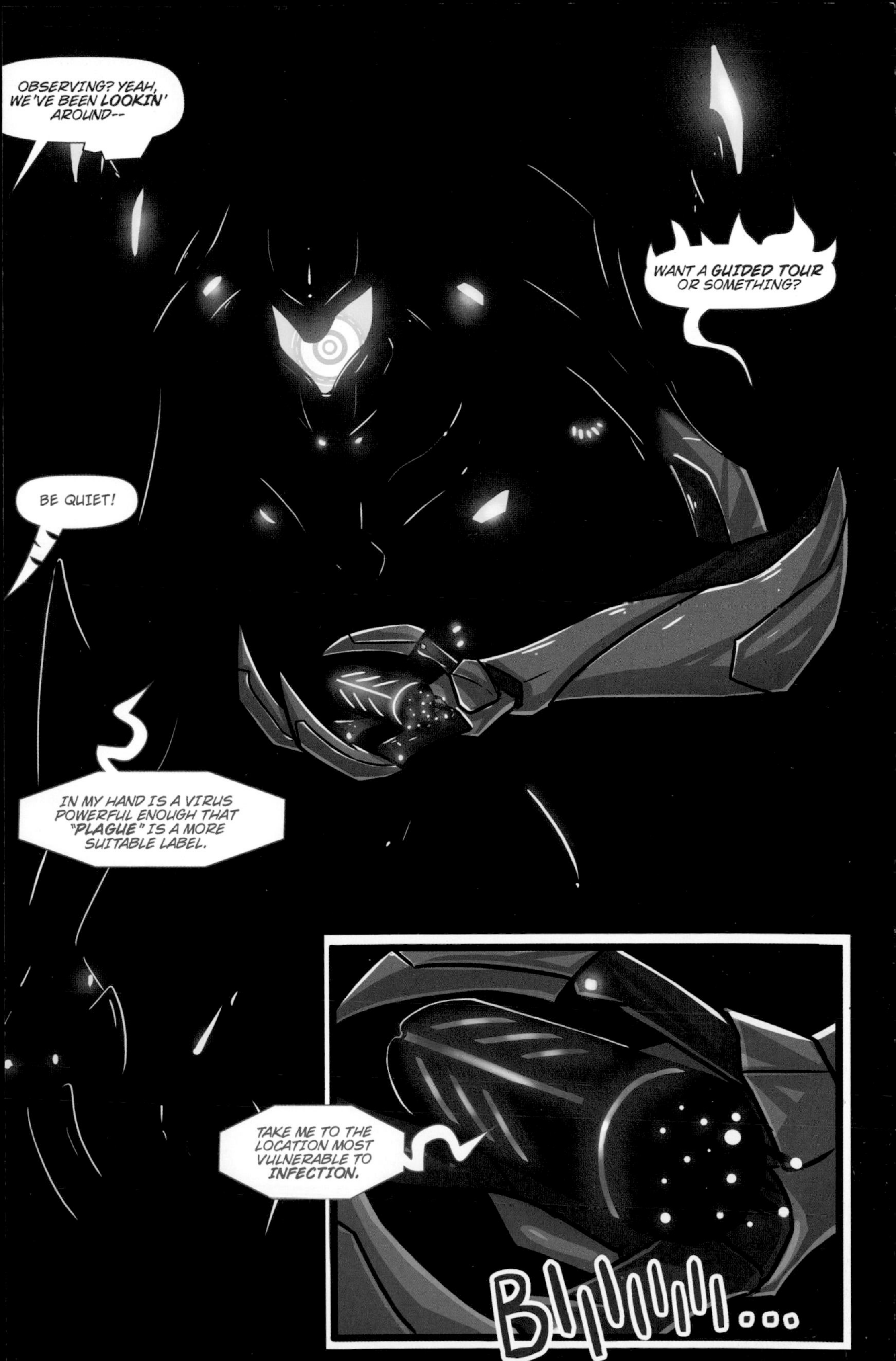

OBSERVING? YEAH, WE'VE BEEN LOOKIN' AROUND--
WANT A GUIDED TOUR OR SOMETHING?
BE QUIET!
IN MY HAND IS A VIRUS POWERFUL ENOUGH THAT "PLAGUE" IS A MORE SUITABLE LABEL.
TAKE ME TO THE LOCATION MOST VULNERABLE TO INFECTION.
BIIIIII...

• HAYWIRE •

CHAPTER 2
GOING VIRAL

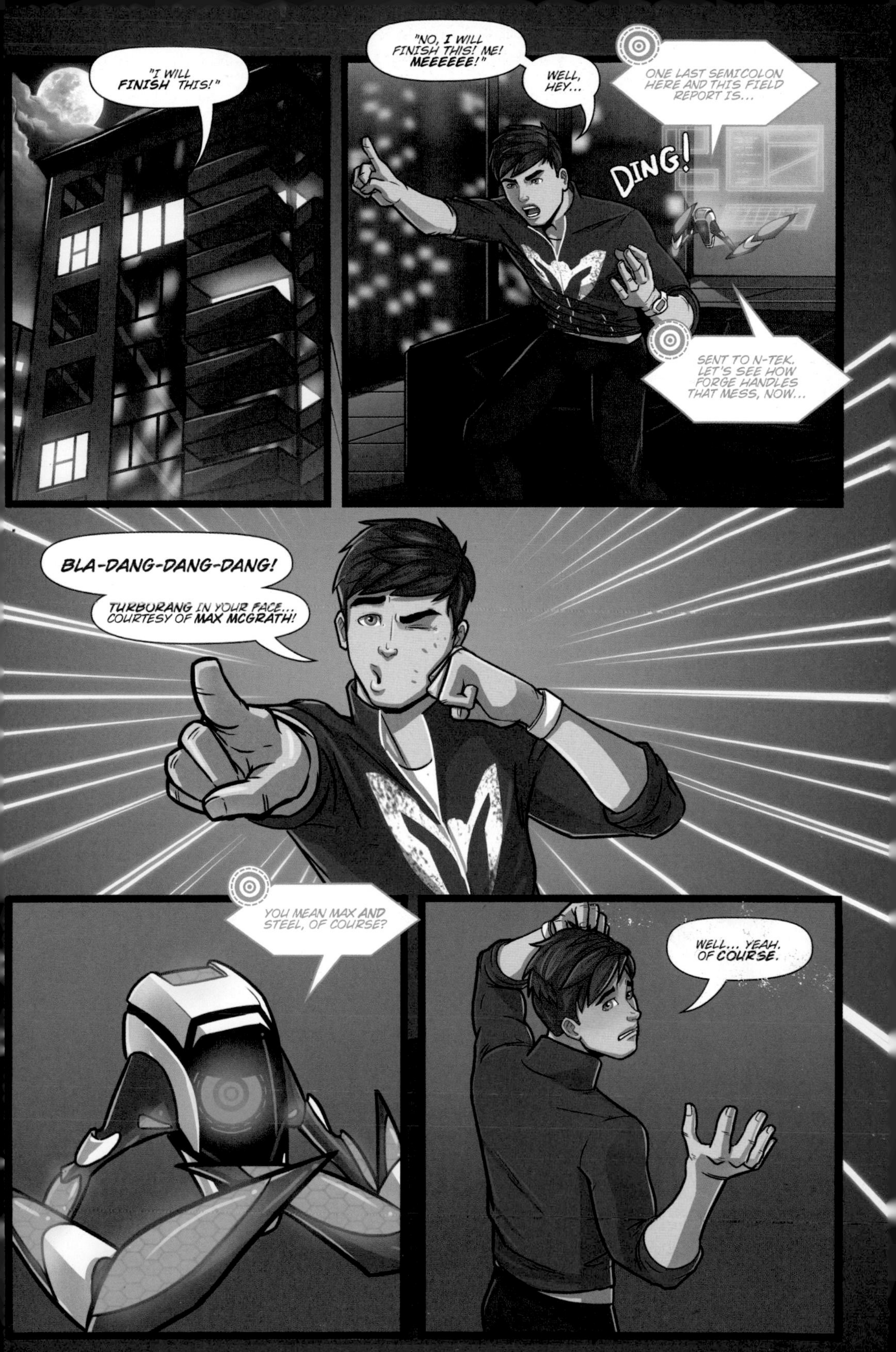
"I WILL FINISH THIS!"
"NO, I WILL FINISH THIS! ME! MEEEEEE!"
WELL, HEY...
ONE LAST SEMICOLON HERE AND THIS FIELD REPORT IS...
DING!
SENT TO N-TEK. LET'S SEE HOW FORGE HANDLES THAT MESS, NOW...
BLA-DANG-DANG-DANG!
TURBORANG IN YOUR FACE... COURTESY OF MAX MCGRATH!
YOU MEAN MAX AND STEEL, OF COURSE?
WELL... YEAH. OF COURSE.

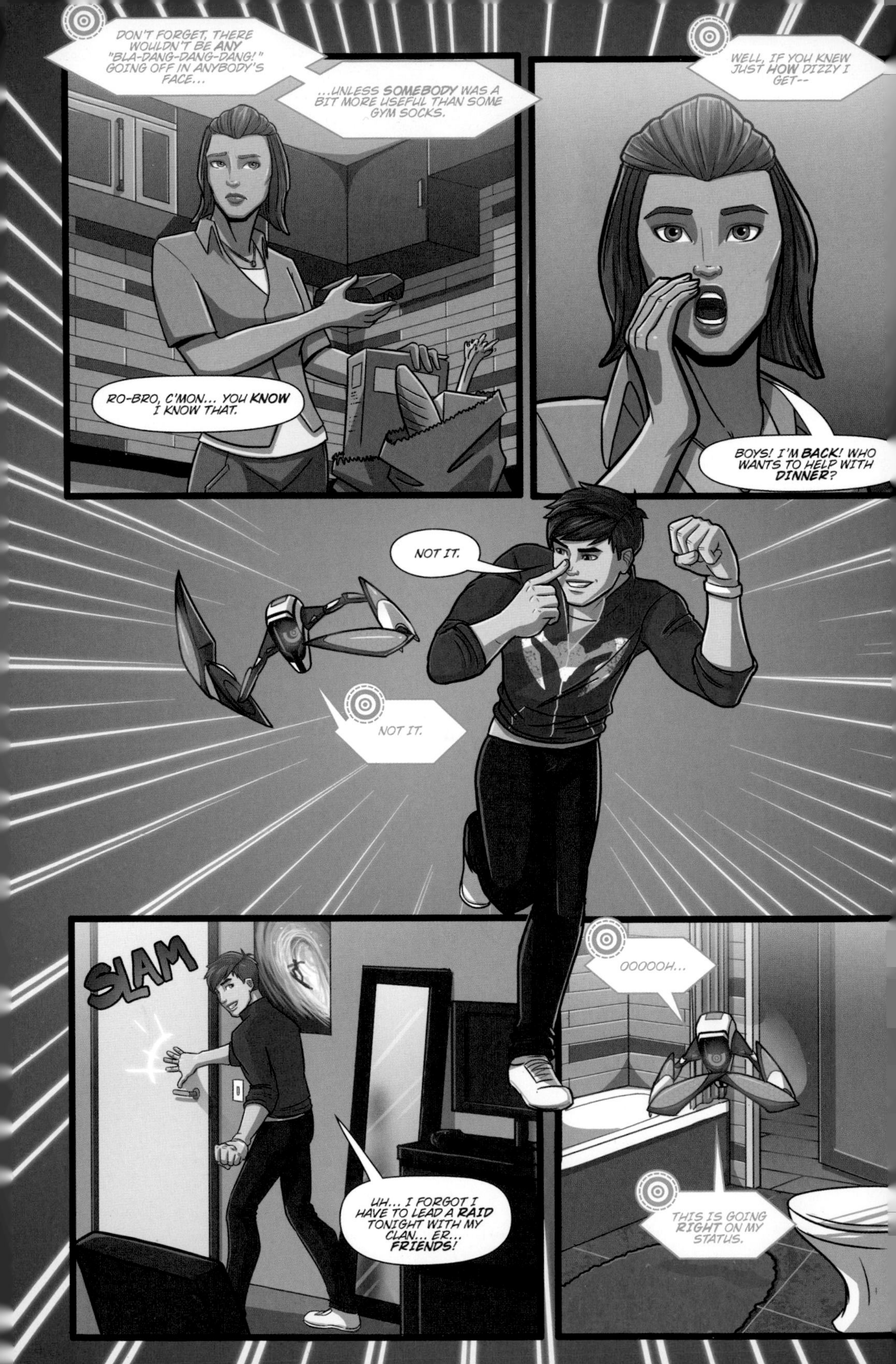
DON'T FORGET, THERE WOULDN'T BE ANY "BLA-DANG-DANG-DANG!" GOING OFF IN ANYBODY'S FACE...
...UNLESS SOMEBODY WAS A BIT MORE USEFUL THAN SOME GYM SOCKS.
RO-BRO, C'MON... YOU KNOW I KNOW THAT.
WELL, IF YOU KNEW JUST HOW DIZZY I GET--
BOYS! I'M BACK! WHO WANTS TO HELP WITH DINNER?
NOT IT.
NOT IT.
SLAM
UH... I FORGOT I HAVE TO LEAD A RAID TONIGHT WITH MY CLAN... ER... FRIENDS!
OOOOOH...
THIS IS GOING RIGHT ON MY STATUS.

JOINING FANTASTIC FRIENDS CO-OP CAMPAIGN...

SID, I NEED YOU TO SHOCK THAT **POWER GENERATOR** OUT!

MAX

ALL **RIGHT**, GUYS...

LET'S SHOW THESE JOKERS HOW IT'S **DONE**.

YOU **GOT IT**, MAX!

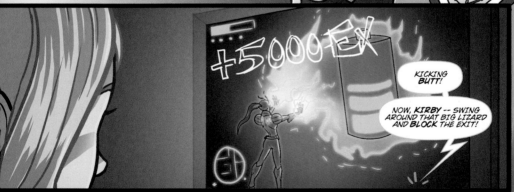

+5000EX

KICKING **BUTT**!

NOW, **KIRBY** -- SWING AROUND THAT BIG LIZARD AND **BLOCK THE EXIT**!

UH, GUYS... ANYBODY ELSE GETTING SOME **MAJOR LAG** RIGHT NOW?

SEARCHING FOR HOST

KIRBY

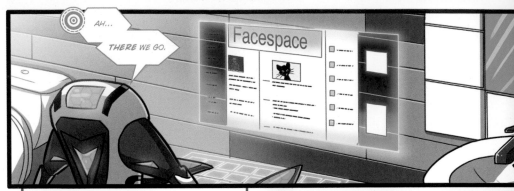

AH...

THERE WE GO.

Facespace

Stellan's status
"So who else was underappreciated today?" 👍 5

Sam: "Oh no what happened? Call me if you need to talk."

Mike: "Feeling EXACTLY like that! LOL"

HUH?

NOW, THAT HASN'T RUNG IN A LONG WHILE.

RING RING RING

CALL

!
FACESPACE IS EXPERIENCING SOME TECHNICA DIFFICULTIES APOLOGIES

WHAT? NO!

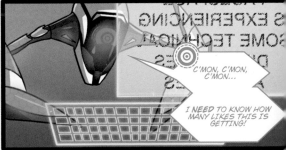

C'MON, C'MON, C'MON...

I NEED TO KNOW HOW MANY LIKES THIS IS GETTING!

HELLO...?

MOLLY -- IT'S FORGE! TURN ON YOUR TV RIGHT NOW!

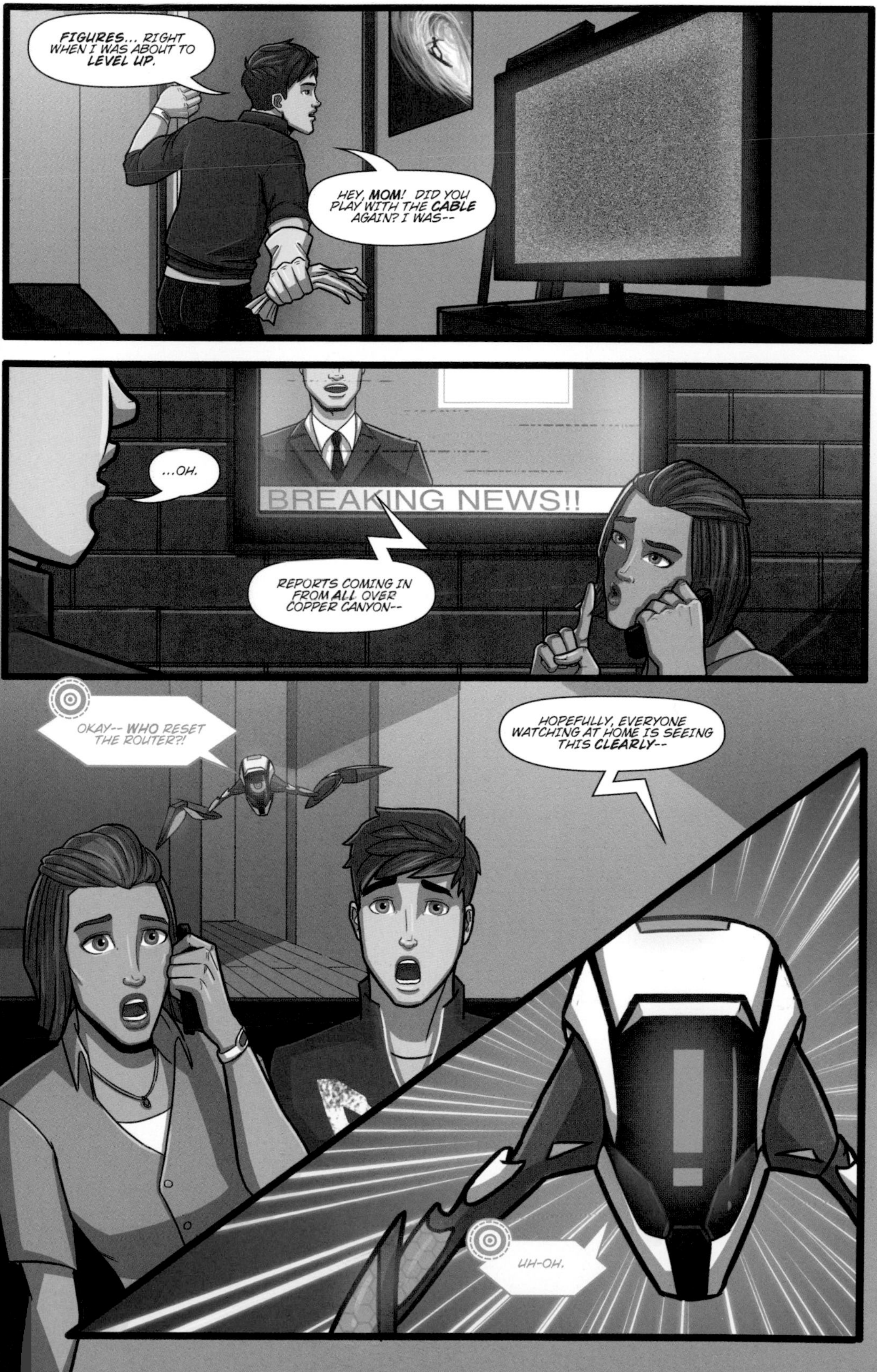
FIGURES... RIGHT WHEN I WAS ABOUT TO LEVEL UP.
HEY, MOM! DID YOU PLAY WITH THE CABLE AGAIN? I WAS--
...OH.
BREAKING NEWS!!
REPORTS COMING IN FROM ALL OVER COPPER CANYON--
OKAY-- WHO RESET THE ROUTER?!
HOPEFULLY, EVERYONE WATCHING AT HOME IS SEEING THIS CLEARLY--
UH-OH.

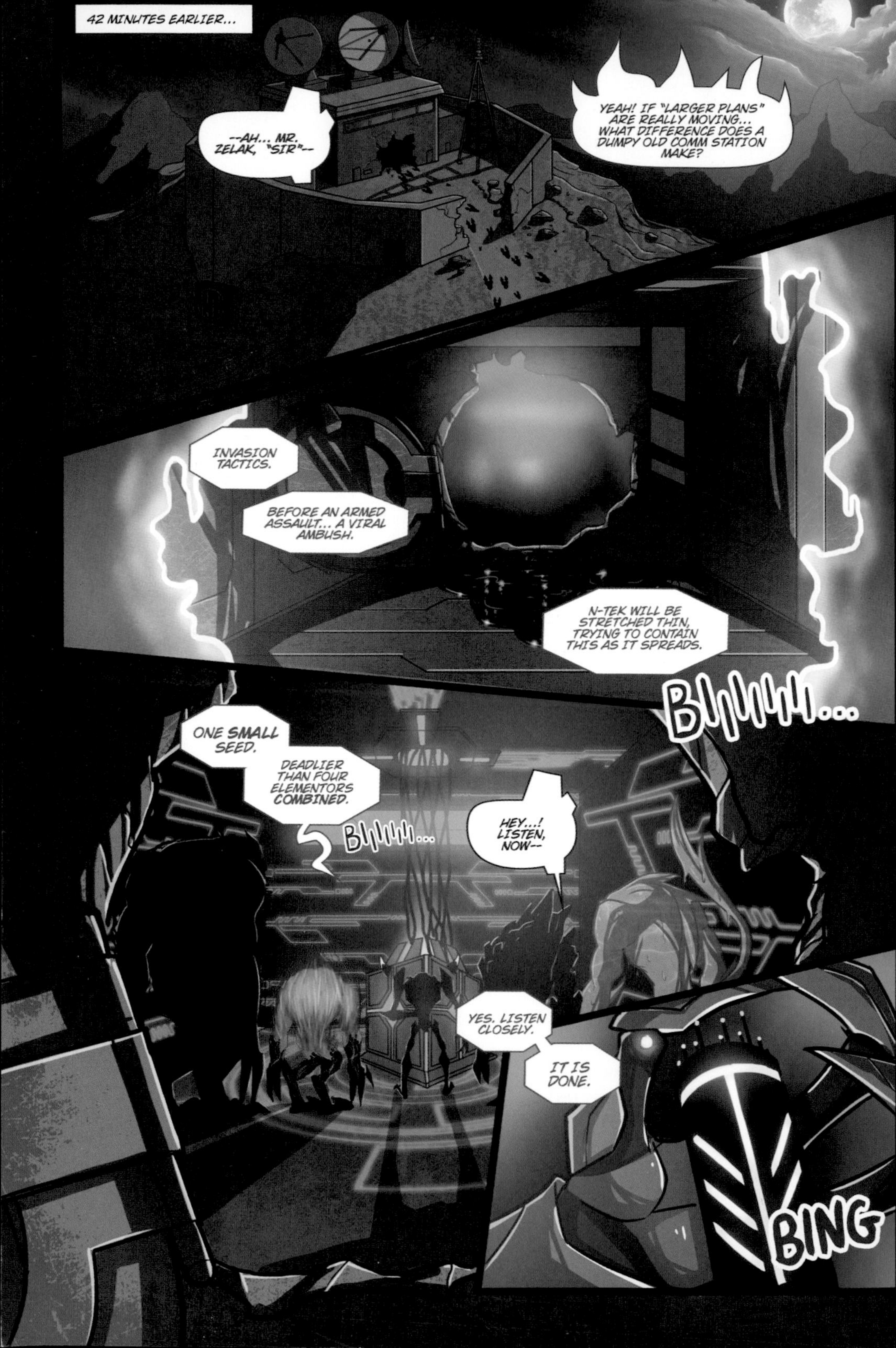
42 MINUTES EARLIER...
--AH... MR. ZELAK, "SIR"--
YEAH! IF "LARGER PLANS" ARE REALLY MOVING... WHAT DIFFERENCE DOES A DUMPY OLD COMM STATION MAKE?
INVASION TACTICS.
BEFORE AN ARMED ASSAULT... A VIRAL AMBUSH.
N-TEK WILL BE STRETCHED THIN, TRYING TO CONTAIN THIS AS IT SPREADS.
BIIIIIII...
ONE SMALL SEED.
DEADLIER THAN FOUR ELEMENTORS COMBINED.
BIIIII...
HEY...! LISTEN, NOW--
YES. LISTEN CLOSELY.
IT IS DONE.
BING

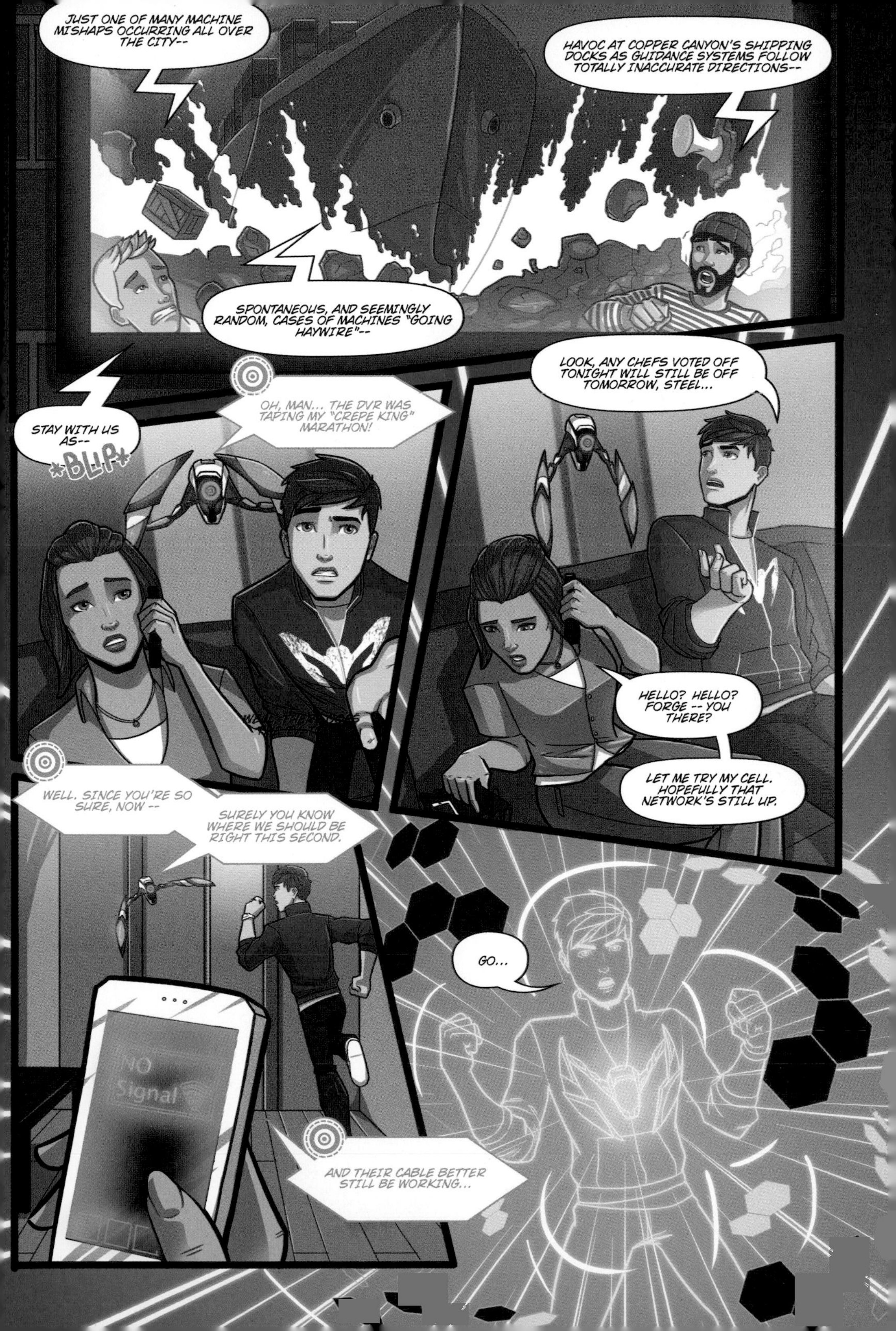

JUST ONE OF MANY MACHINE MISHAPS OCCURRING ALL OVER THE CITY--
HAVOC AT COPPER CANYON'S SHIPPING DOCKS AS GUIDANCE SYSTEMS FOLLOW TOTALLY INACCURATE DIRECTIONS--
SPONTANEOUS, AND SEEMINGLY RANDOM, CASES OF MACHINES "GOING HAYWIRE"--
STAY WITH US AS--
BLIP
OH, MAN... THE DVR WAS TAPING MY "CREPE KING" MARATHON!
LOOK, ANY CHEFS VOTED OFF TONIGHT WILL STILL BE OFF TOMORROW, STEEL...
HELLO? HELLO? FORGE -- YOU THERE?
LET ME TRY MY CELL. HOPEFULLY THAT NETWORK'S STILL UP.
WELL. SINCE YOU'RE SO SURE, NOW --
SURELY YOU KNOW WHERE WE SHOULD BE RIGHT THIS SECOND.
GO...
NO Signal
AND THEIR CABLE BETTER STILL BE WORKING...

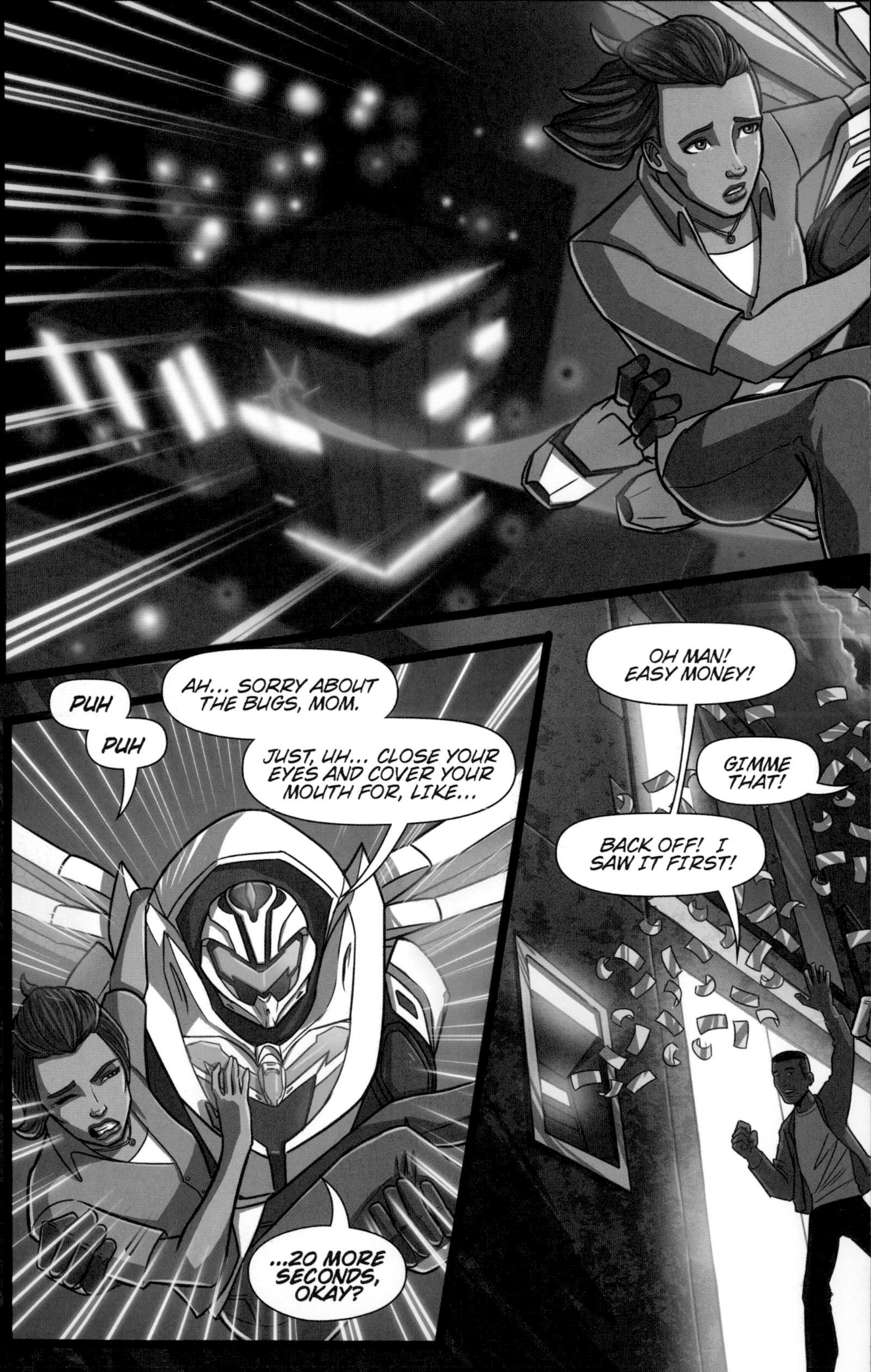
PUH
PUH
AH... SORRY ABOUT THE BUGS, MOM.
JUST, UH... CLOSE YOUR EYES AND COVER YOUR MOUTH FOR, LIKE...
...20 MORE SECONDS, OKAY?
OH MAN! EASY MONEY!
GIMME THAT!
BACK OFF! I SAW IT FIRST!

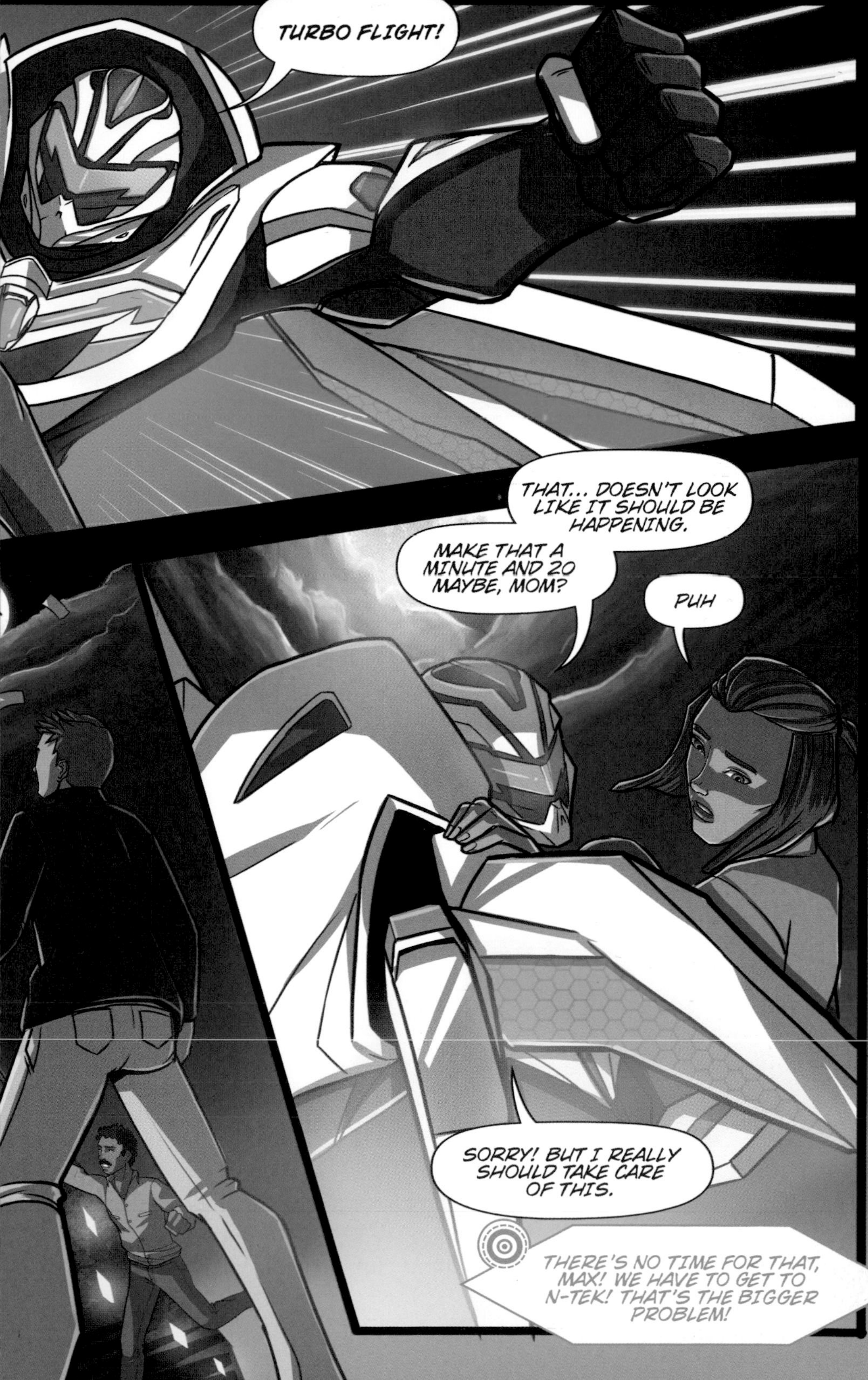
TURBO FLIGHT!
THAT... DOESN'T LOOK LIKE IT SHOULD BE HAPPENING.
MAKE THAT A MINUTE AND 20 MAYBE, MOM?
PUH
SORRY! BUT I REALLY SHOULD TAKE CARE OF THIS.
THERE'S NO TIME FOR THAT, MAX! WE HAVE TO GET TO N-TEK! THAT'S THE BIGGER PROBLEM!

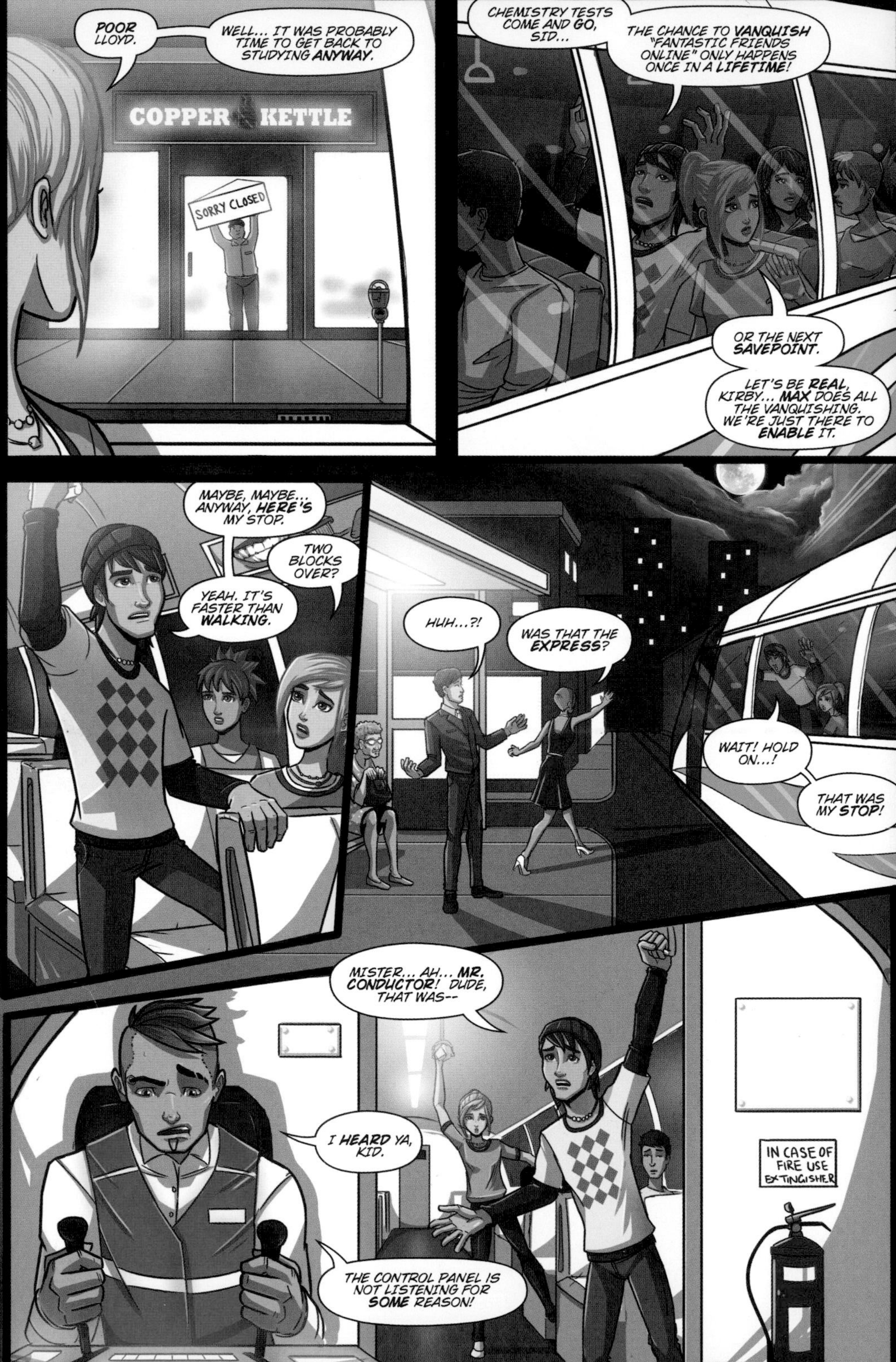
POOR LLOYD.
WELL... IT WAS PROBABLY TIME TO GET BACK TO STUDYING ANYWAY.
COPPER KETTLE
SORRY CLOSED
CHEMISTRY TESTS COME AND GO, SID...
THE CHANCE TO VANQUISH "FANTASTIC FRIENDS ONLINE" ONLY HAPPENS ONCE IN A LIFETIME!
OR THE NEXT SAVEPOINT.
LET'S BE REAL, KIRBY... MAX DOES ALL THE VANQUISHING. WE'RE JUST THERE TO ENABLE IT.
MAYBE, MAYBE... ANYWAY, HERE'S MY STOP.
TWO BLOCKS OVER?
YEAH. IT'S FASTER THAN WALKING.
HUH...?!
WAS THAT THE EXPRESS?
WAIT! HOLD ON...!
THAT WAS MY STOP!
MISTER... AH... MR. CONDUCTOR! DUDE, THAT WAS--
I HEARD YA, KID.
THE CONTROL PANEL IS NOT LISTENING FOR SOME REASON!
IN CASE OF FIRE USE EXTINGISHER

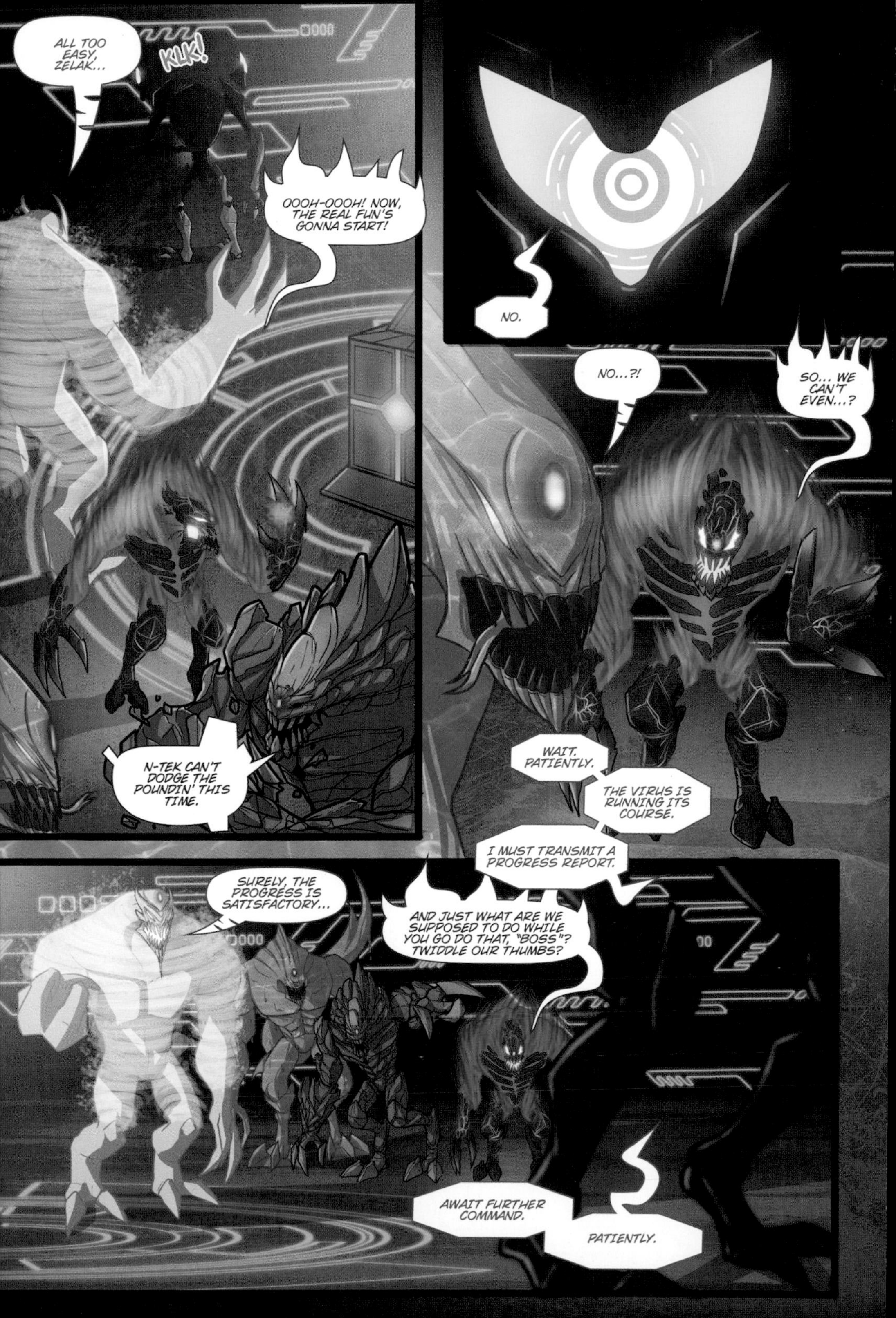
ALL TOO EASY, ZELAK...
KLK!
OOOH-OOOH! NOW, THE REAL FUN'S GONNA START!
N-TEK CAN'T DODGE THE POUNDIN' THIS TIME.
NO.
NO...?!
SO... WE CAN'T EVEN...?
WAIT. PATIENTLY.
THE VIRUS IS RUNNING ITS COURSE.
I MUST TRANSMIT A PROGRESS REPORT.
SURELY, THE PROGRESS IS SATISFACTORY...
AND JUST WHAT ARE WE SUPPOSED TO DO WHILE YOU GO DO THAT, "BOSS"? TWIDDLE OUR THUMBS?
AWAIT FURTHER COMMAND.
PATIENTLY.

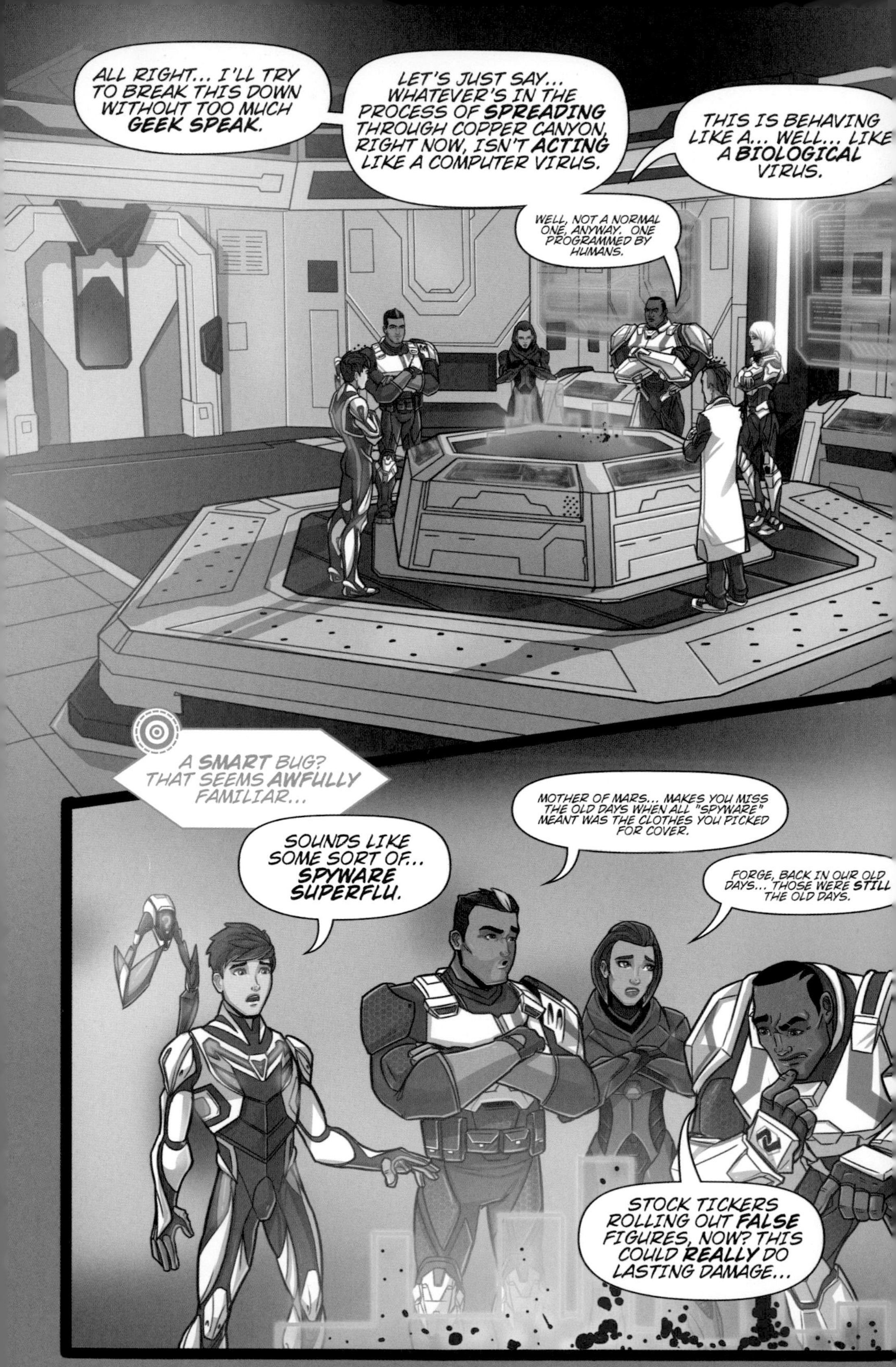
ALL RIGHT... I'LL TRY TO BREAK THIS DOWN WITHOUT TOO MUCH GEEK SPEAK.
LET'S JUST SAY... WHATEVER'S IN THE PROCESS OF SPREADING THROUGH COPPER CANYON, RIGHT NOW, ISN'T ACTING LIKE A COMPUTER VIRUS.
THIS IS BEHAVING LIKE A... WELL... LIKE A BIOLOGICAL VIRUS.
WELL, NOT A NORMAL ONE, ANYWAY. ONE PROGRAMMED BY HUMANS.
A SMART BUG? THAT SEEMS AWFULLY FAMILIAR...
SOUNDS LIKE SOME SORT OF... SPYWARE SUPERFLU.
MOTHER OF MARS... MAKES YOU MISS THE OLD DAYS WHEN ALL "SPYWARE" MEANT WAS THE CLOTHES YOU PICKED FOR COVER.
FORGE, BACK IN OUR OLD DAYS... THOSE WERE STILL THE OLD DAYS.
STOCK TICKERS ROLLING OUT FALSE FIGURES, NOW? THIS COULD REALLY DO LASTING DAMAGE...

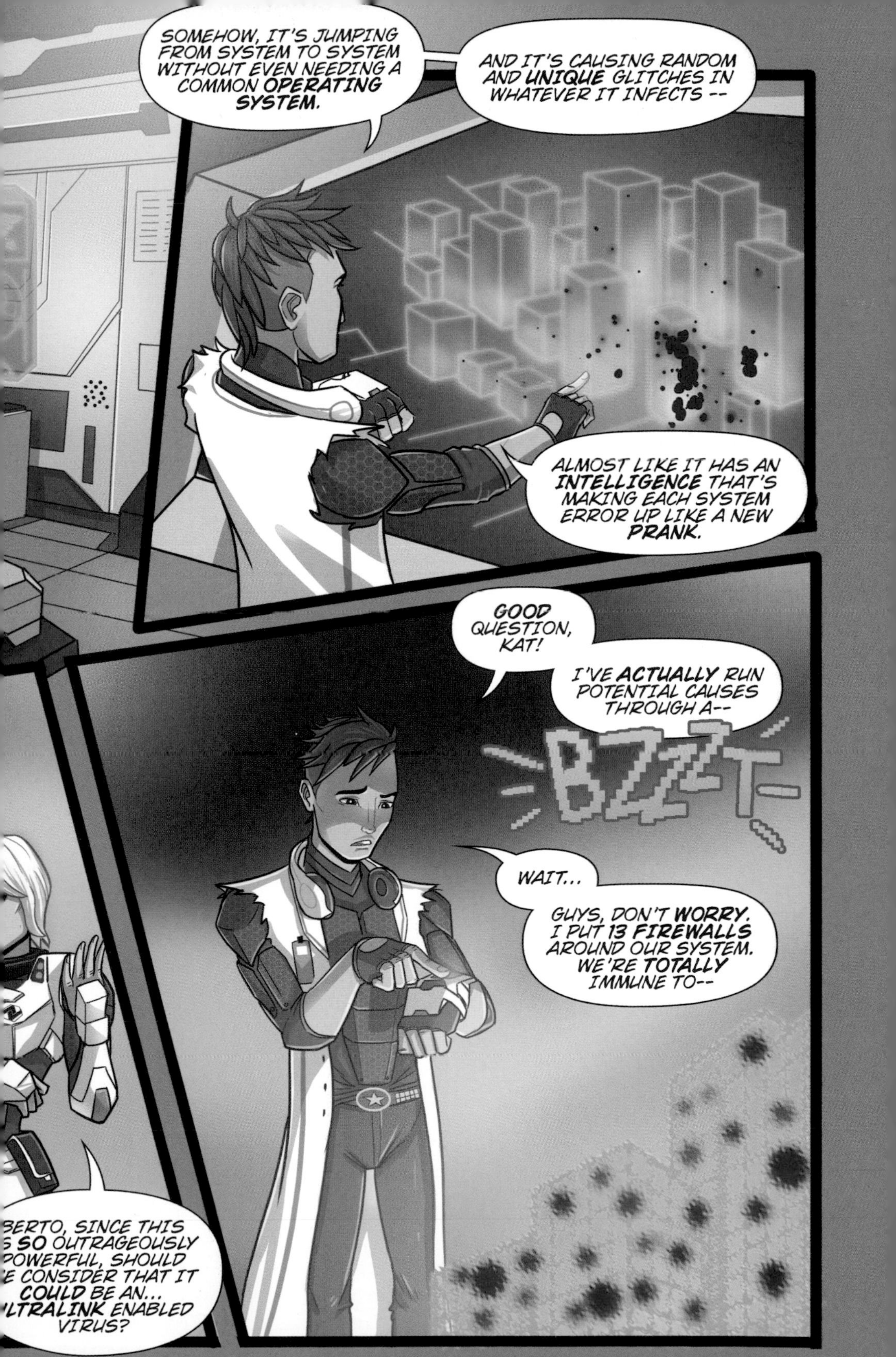
SOMEHOW, IT'S JUMPING FROM SYSTEM TO SYSTEM WITHOUT EVEN NEEDING A COMMON OPERATING SYSTEM.
AND IT'S CAUSING RANDOM AND UNIQUE GLITCHES IN WHATEVER IT INFECTS --
ALMOST LIKE IT HAS AN INTELLIGENCE THAT'S MAKING EACH SYSTEM ERROR UP LIKE A NEW PRANK.
BERTO, SINCE THIS S SO OUTRAGEOUSLY POWERFUL, SHOULD E CONSIDER THAT IT COULD BE AN... LTRALINK ENABLED VIRUS?
GOOD QUESTION, KAT!
I'VE ACTUALLY RUN POTENTIAL CAUSES THROUGH A--
BZZZT
WAIT...
GUYS, DON'T WORRY. I PUT 13 FIREWALLS AROUND OUR SYSTEM. WE'RE TOTALLY IMMUNE TO--

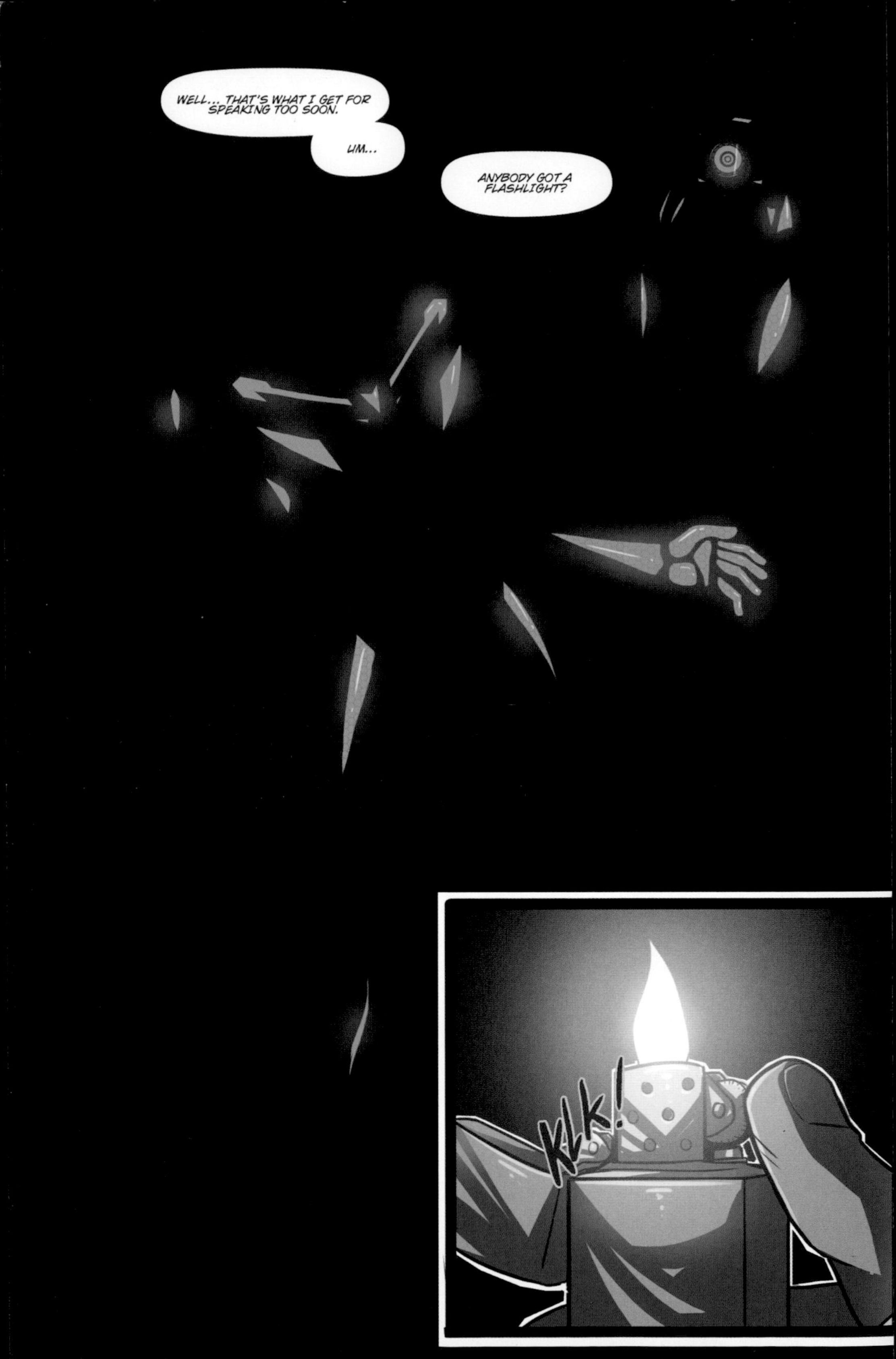
WELL... THAT'S WHAT I GET FOR SPEAKING TOO SOON.
UM...
ANYBODY GOT A FLASHLIGHT?
KLIK!

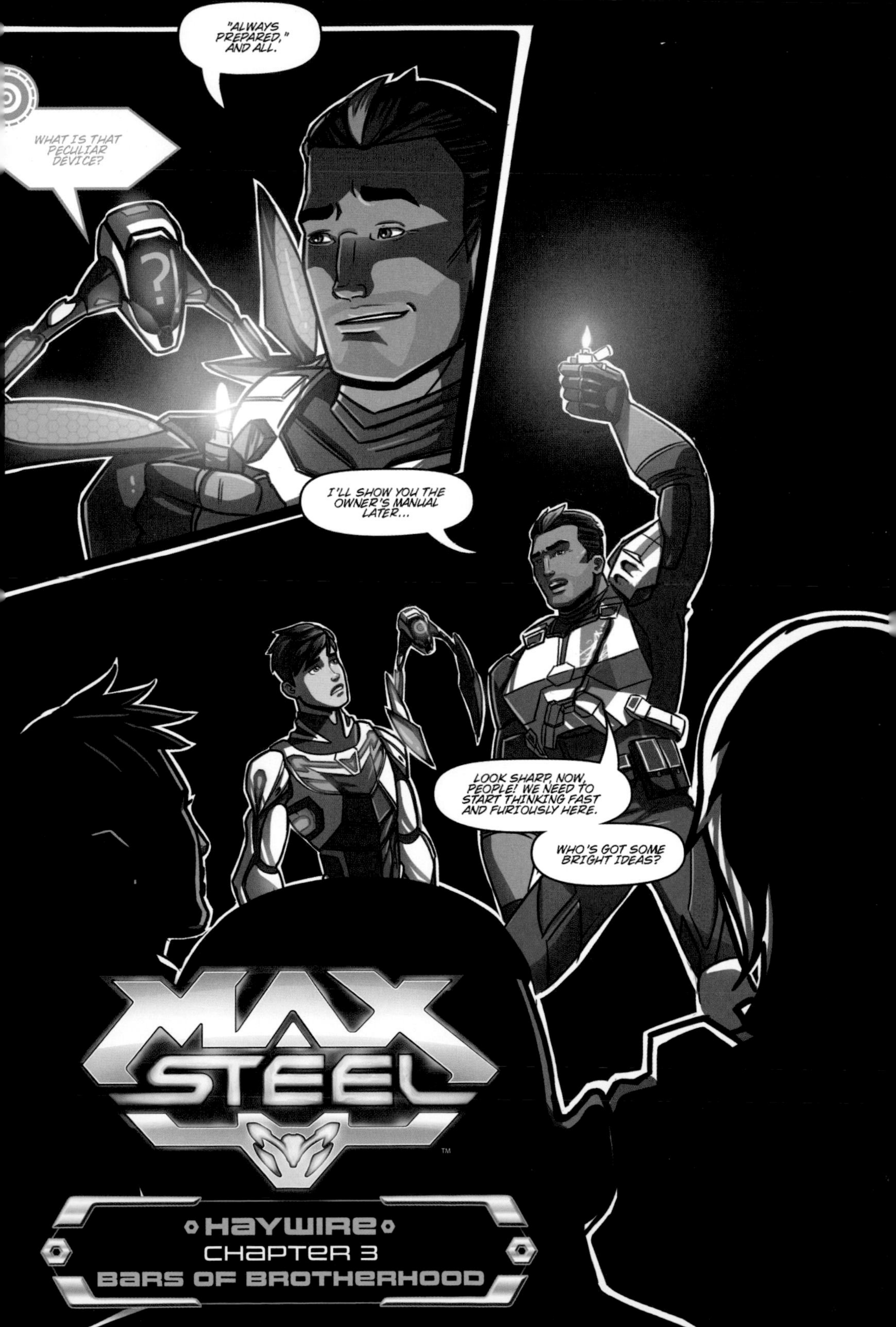
WHAT IS THAT PECULIAR DEVICE?
"ALWAYS PREPARED," AND ALL.
I'LL SHOW YOU THE OWNER'S MANUAL LATER...
LOOK SHARP, NOW, PEOPLE! WE NEED TO START THINKING FAST AND FURIOUSLY HERE.
WHO'S GOT SOME BRIGHT IDEAS?
MAX STEEL
TM
HAYWIRE
CHAPTER 3
BARS OF BROTHERHOOD

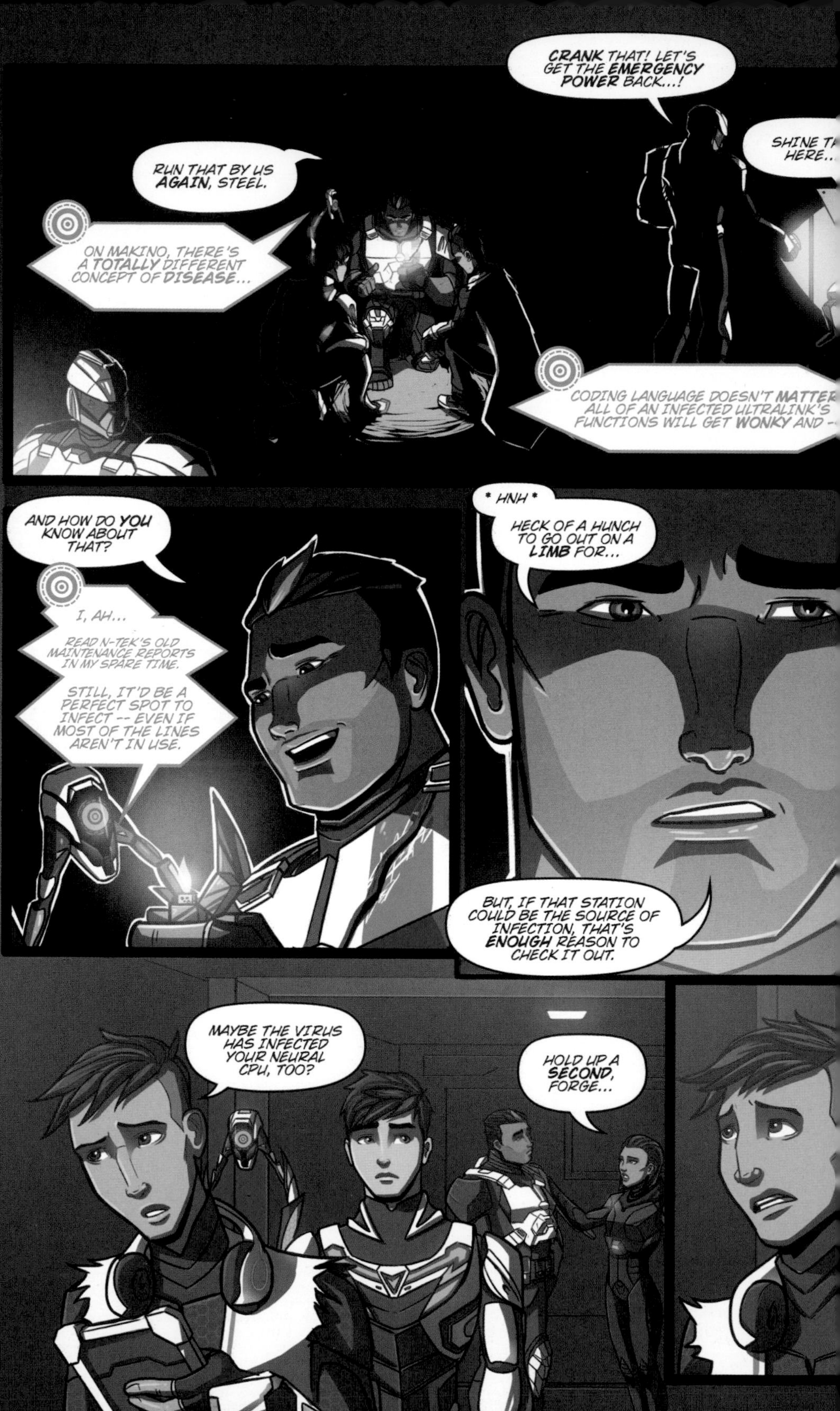

RUN THAT BY US AGAIN, STEEL.
ON MAKINO, THERE'S A TOTALLY DIFFERENT CONCEPT OF DISEASE...
CRANK THAT! LET'S GET THE EMERGENCY POWER BACK...!
SHINE TH HERE...
CODING LANGUAGE DOESN'T MATTER ALL OF AN INFECTED ULTRALINK'S FUNCTIONS WILL GET WONKY AND --
AND HOW DO YOU KNOW ABOUT THAT?
I, AH...
READ N-TEK'S OLD MAINTENANCE REPORTS IN MY SPARE TIME.
STILL, IT'D BE A PERFECT SPOT TO INFECT -- EVEN IF MOST OF THE LINES AREN'T IN USE.
* HNH *
HECK OF A HUNCH TO GO OUT ON A LIMB FOR...
BUT, IF THAT STATION COULD BE THE SOURCE OF INFECTION, THAT'S ENOUGH REASON TO CHECK IT OUT.
MAYBE THE VIRUS HAS INFECTED YOUR NEURAL CPU, TOO?
HOLD UP A SECOND, FORGE...

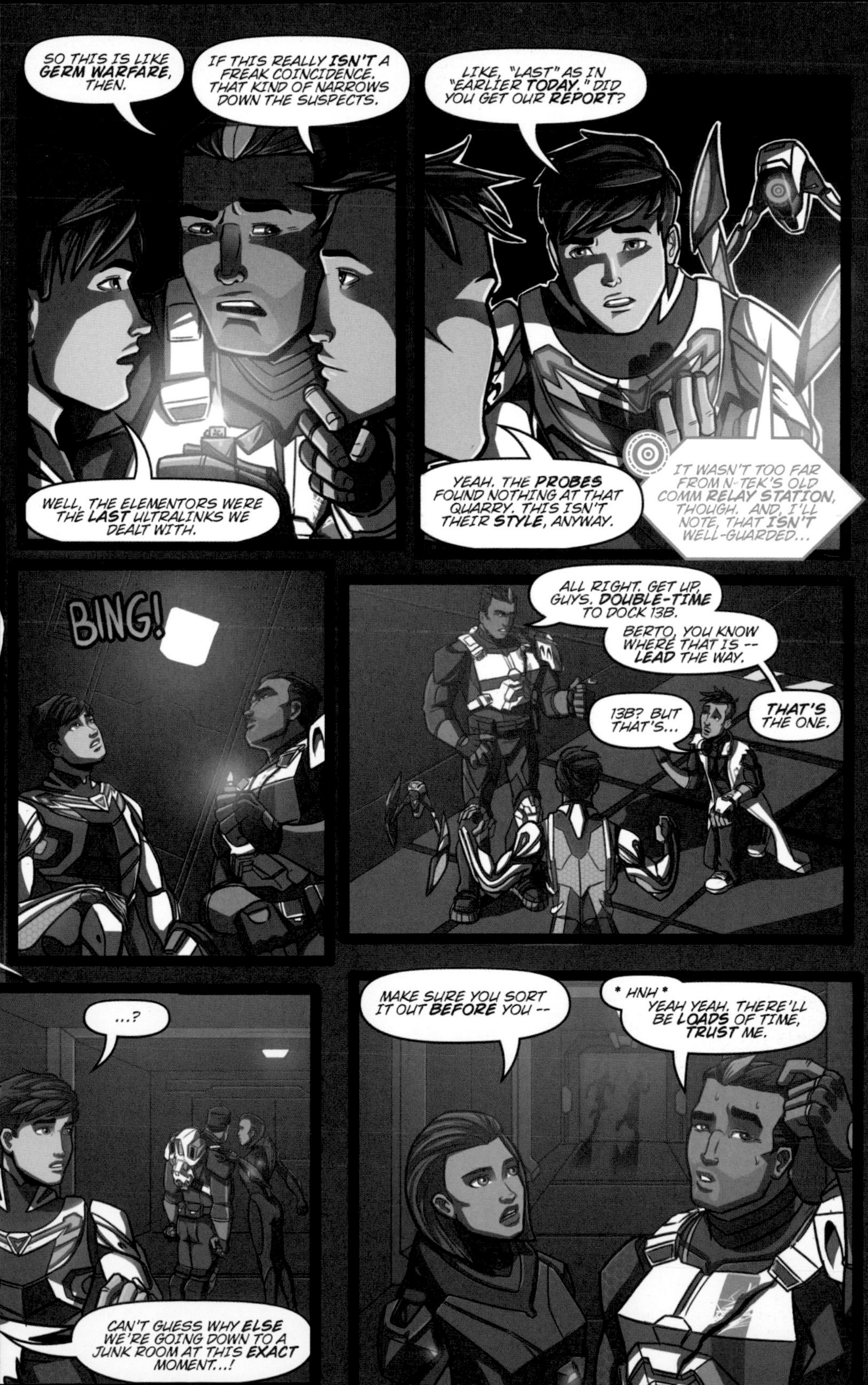
SO THIS IS LIKE GERM WARFARE, THEN.
IF THIS REALLY ISN'T A FREAK COINCIDENCE. THAT KIND OF NARROWS DOWN THE SUSPECTS.
WELL, THE ELEMENTORS WERE THE LAST ULTRALINKS WE DEALT WITH.
LIKE, "LAST" AS IN "EARLIER TODAY." DID YOU GET OUR REPORT?
YEAH. THE PROBES FOUND NOTHING AT THAT QUARRY. THIS ISN'T THEIR STYLE, ANYWAY.
IT WASN'T TOO FAR FROM N-TEK'S OLD COMM RELAY STATION, THOUGH. AND, I'LL NOTE, THAT ISN'T WELL-GUARDED...
BING!
ALL RIGHT. GET UP, GUYS. DOUBLE-TIME TO DOCK 13B.
BERTO, YOU KNOW WHERE THAT IS -- LEAD THE WAY.
13B? BUT THAT'S...
THAT'S THE ONE.
...?
CAN'T GUESS WHY ELSE WE'RE GOING DOWN TO A JUNK ROOM AT THIS EXACT MOMENT...!
MAKE SURE YOU SORT IT OUT BEFORE YOU --
* HNH *
YEAH YEAH. THERE'LL BE LOADS OF TIME, TRUST ME.

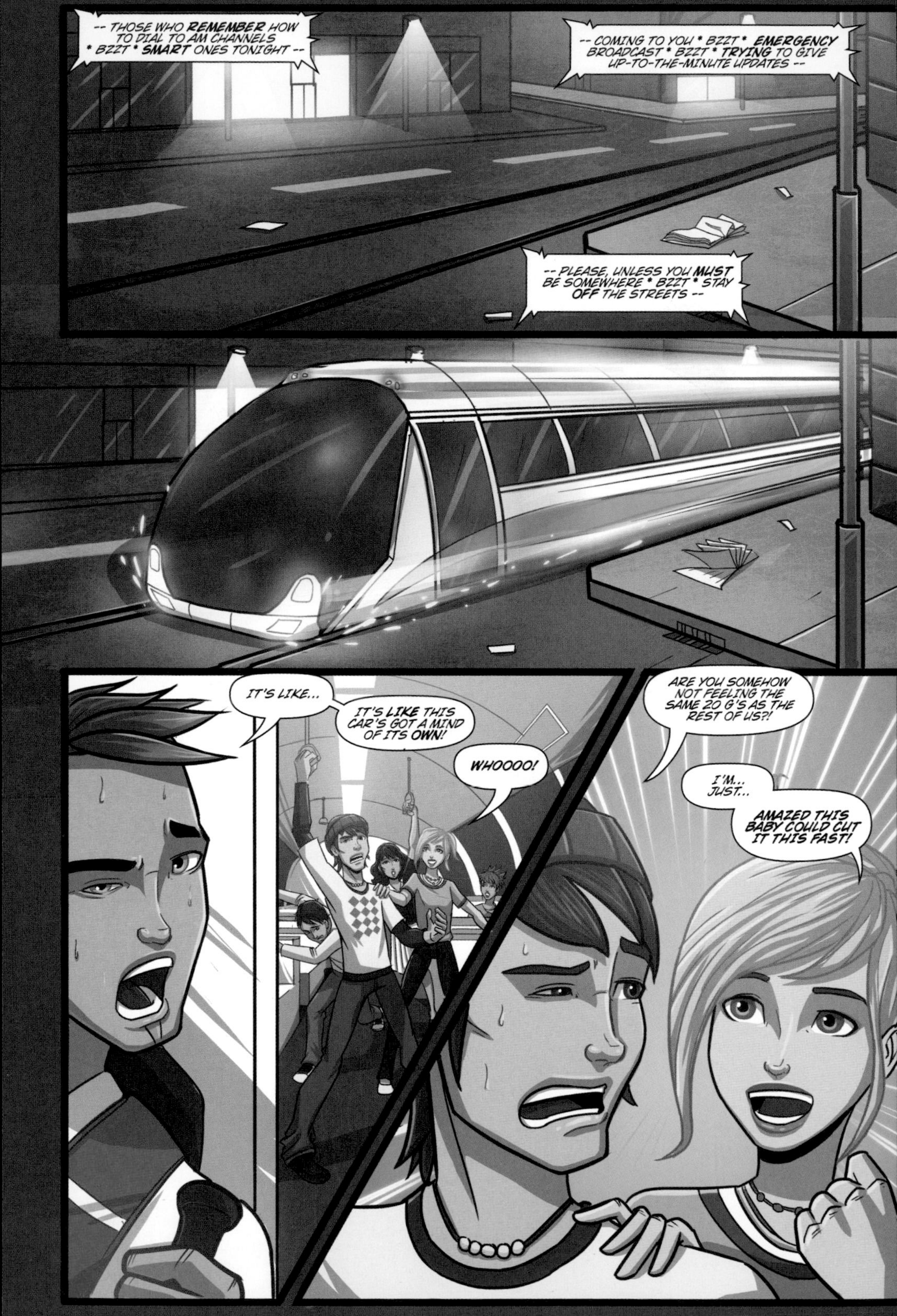
-- THOSE WHO REMEMBER HOW TO DIAL TO AM CHANNELS * BZZT * SMART ONES TONIGHT --
-- COMING TO YOU * BZZT * EMERGENCY BROADCAST * BZZT * TRYING TO GIVE UP-TO-THE-MINUTE UPDATES --
-- PLEASE, UNLESS YOU MUST BE SOMEWHERE * BZZT * STAY OFF THE STREETS --
IT'S LIKE...
IT'S LIKE THIS CAR'S GOT A MIND OF ITS OWN!
WHOOOO!
ARE YOU SOMEHOW NOT FEELING THE SAME 20 G'S AS THE REST OF US?!
I'M... JUST...
AMAZED THIS BABY COULD CUT IT THIS FAST!

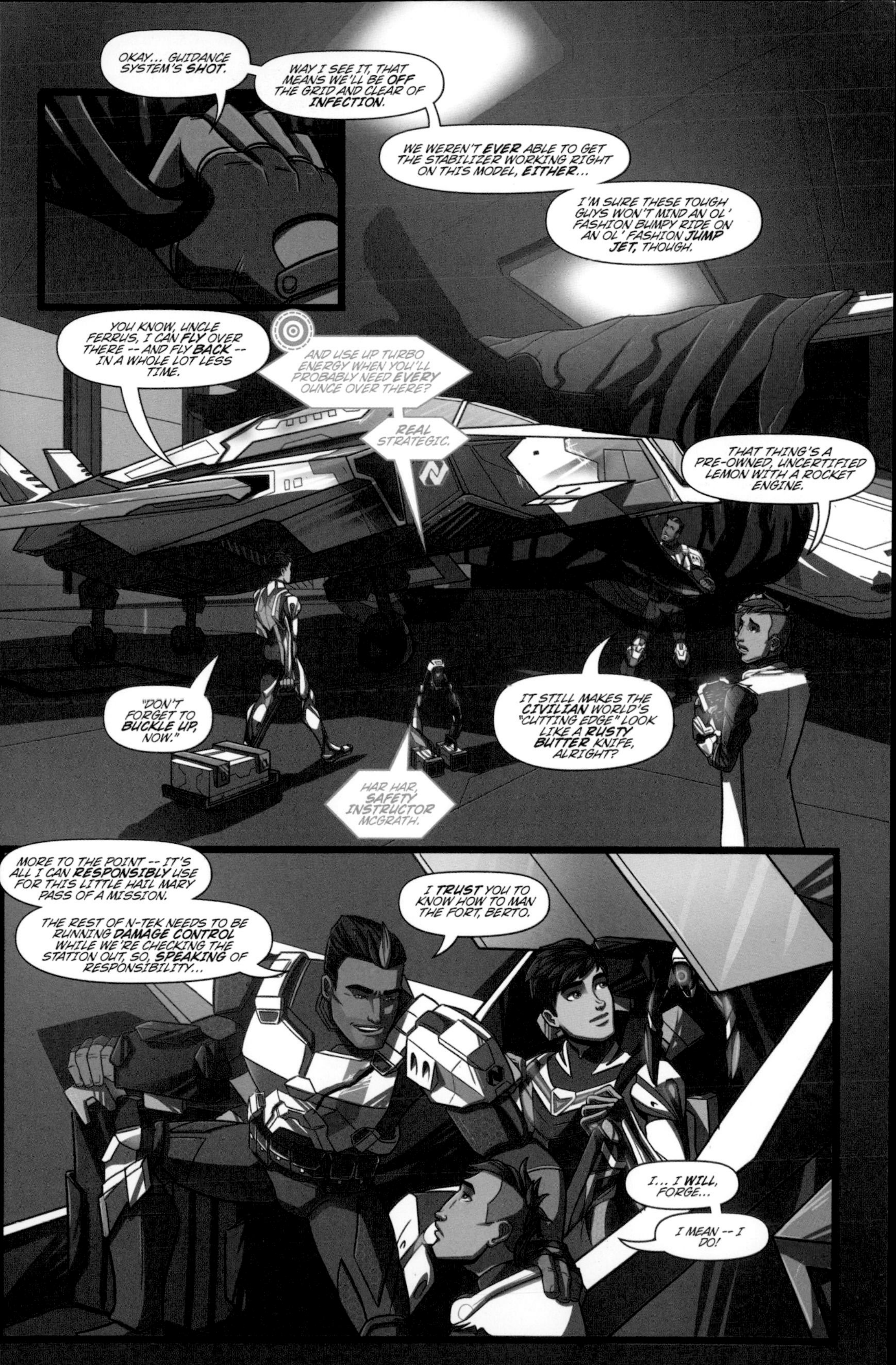
OKAY... GUIDANCE SYSTEM'S SHOT.
WAY I SEE IT, THAT MEANS WE'LL BE OFF THE GRID AND CLEAR OF INFECTION.
WE WEREN'T EVER ABLE TO GET THE STABILIZER WORKING RIGHT ON THIS MODEL, EITHER...
I'M SURE THESE TOUGH GUYS WON'T MIND AN OL' FASHION BUMPY RIDE ON AN OL' FASHION JUMP JET, THOUGH.
YOU KNOW, UNCLE FERRUS, I CAN FLY OVER THERE -- AND FLY BACK -- IN A WHOLE LOT LESS TIME.
AND USE UP TURBO ENERGY WHEN YOU'LL PROBABLY NEED EVERY OUNCE OVER THERE?
REAL STRATEGIC.
THAT THING'S A PRE-OWNED, UNCERTIFIED LEMON WITH A ROCKET ENGINE.
"DON'T FORGET TO BUCKLE UP, NOW."
HAR HAR, SAFETY INSTRUCTOR MCGRATH.
IT STILL MAKES THE CIVILIAN WORLD'S "CUTTING EDGE" LOOK LIKE A RUSTY BUTTER KNIFE, ALRIGHT?
MORE TO THE POINT -- IT'S ALL I CAN RESPONSIBLY USE FOR THIS LITTLE HAIL MARY PASS OF A MISSION.
THE REST OF N-TEK NEEDS TO BE RUNNING DAMAGE CONTROL WHILE WE'RE CHECKING THE STATION OUT, SO, SPEAKING OF RESPONSIBILITY...
I TRUST YOU TO KNOW HOW TO MAN THE FORT, BERTO.
I... I WILL, FORGE...
I MEAN -- I DO!

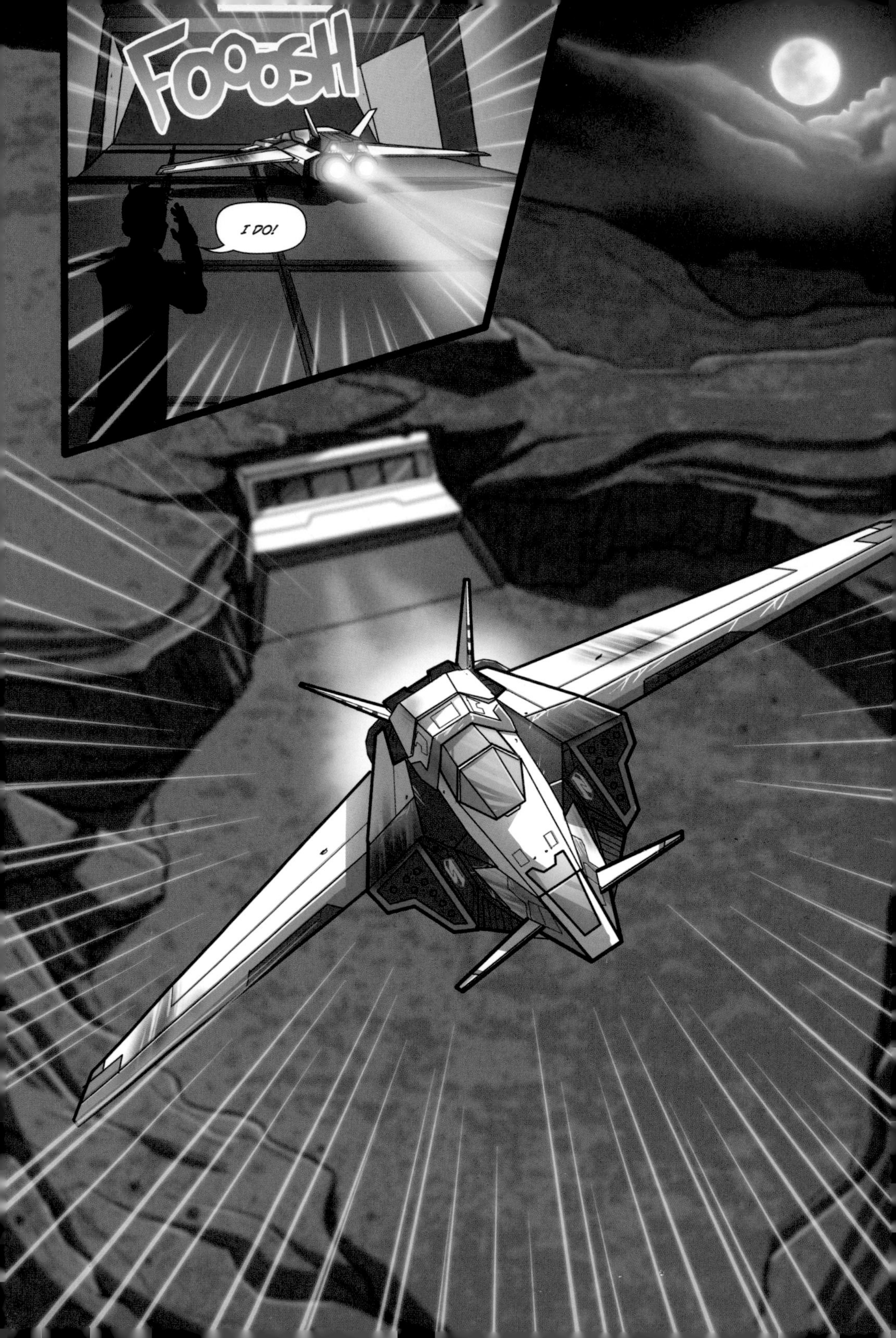
FOOOSH
I DO!

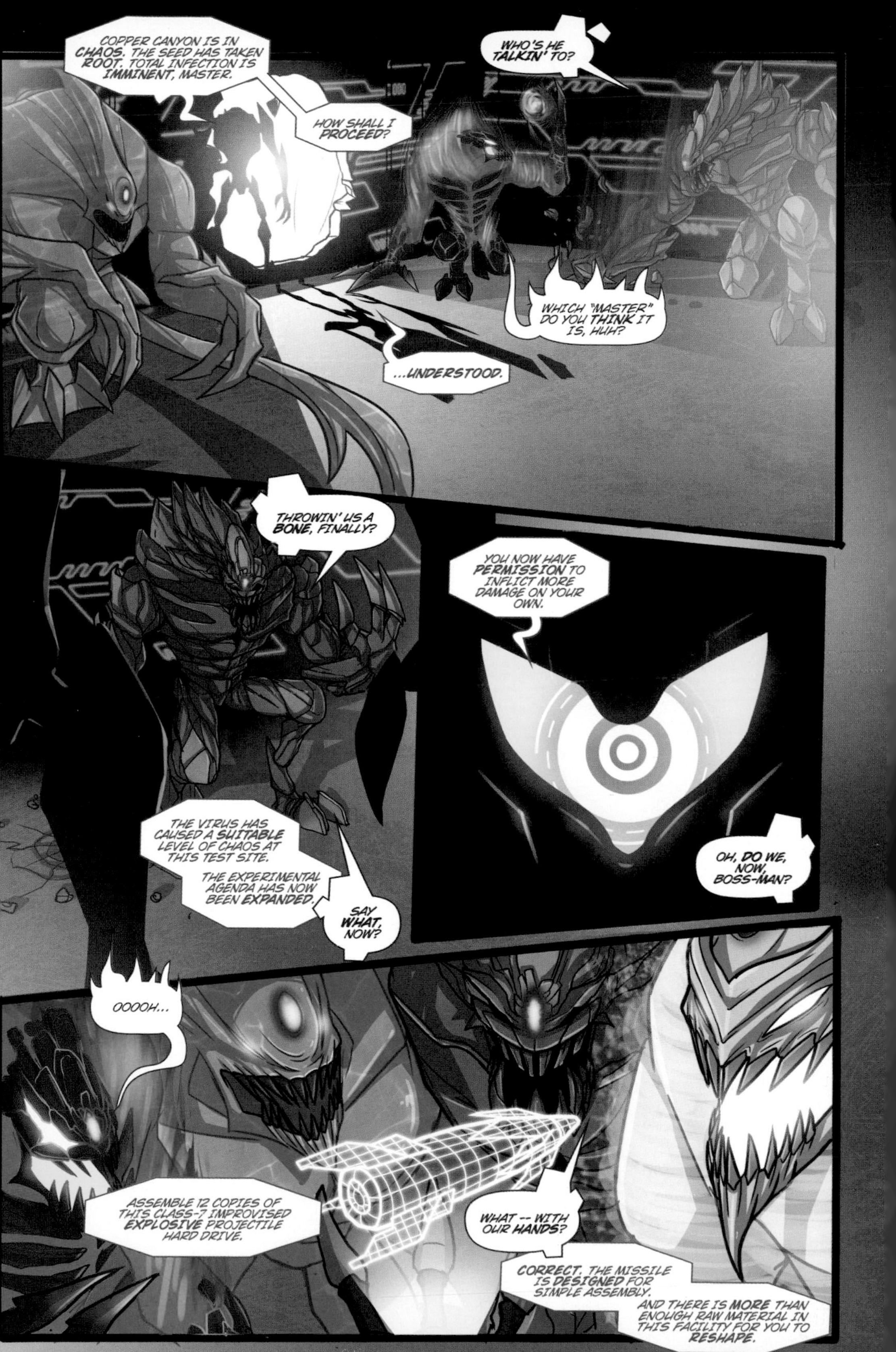

COPPER CANYON IS IN CHAOS. THE SEED HAS TAKEN ROOT. TOTAL INFECTION IS IMMINENT, MASTER.
HOW SHALL I PROCEED?
WHO'S HE TALKIN' TO?
WHICH "MASTER" DO YOU THINK IT IS, HUH?
...UNDERSTOOD.
THROWIN' US A BONE, FINALLY?
YOU NOW HAVE PERMISSION TO INFLICT MORE DAMAGE ON YOUR OWN.
THE VIRUS HAS CAUSED A SUITABLE LEVEL OF CHAOS AT THIS TEST SITE.
THE EXPERIMENTAL AGENDA HAS NOW BEEN EXPANDED.
SAY WHAT, NOW?
OH, DO WE, NOW, BOSS-MAN?
OOOOH...
ASSEMBLE 12 COPIES OF THIS CLASS-7 IMPROVISED EXPLOSIVE PROJECTILE HARD DRIVE.
WHAT -- WITH OUR HANDS?
CORRECT. THE MISSILE IS DESIGNED FOR SIMPLE ASSEMBLY.
AND THERE IS MORE THAN ENOUGH RAW MATERIAL IN THIS FACILITY FOR YOU TO RESHAPE.

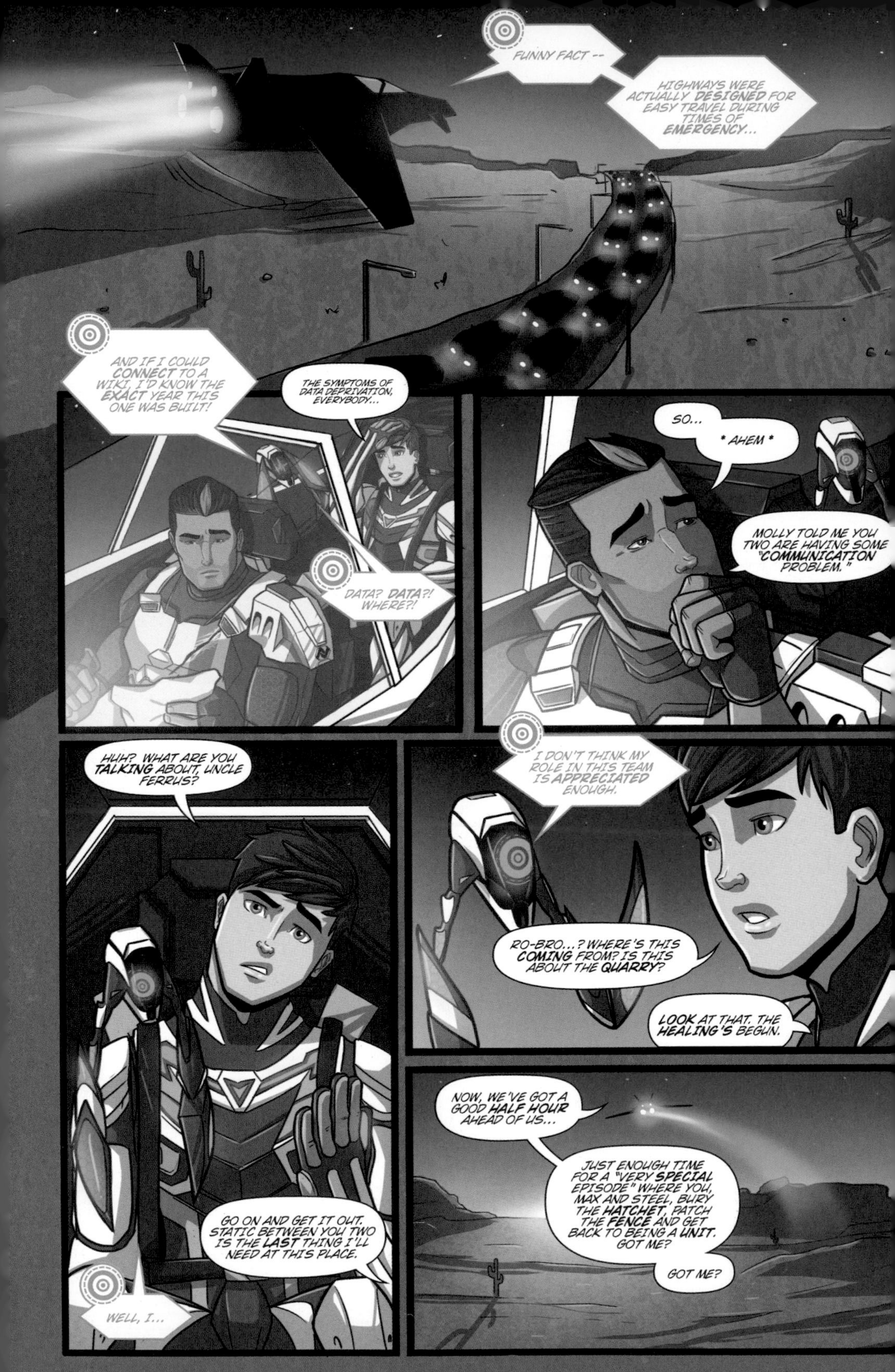
FUNNY FACT --
HIGHWAYS WERE ACTUALLY DESIGNED FOR EASY TRAVEL DURING TIMES OF EMERGENCY...
AND IF I COULD CONNECT TO A WIKI, I'D KNOW THE EXACT YEAR THIS ONE WAS BUILT!
THE SYMPTOMS OF DATA DEPRIVATION, EVERYBODY...
DATA? DATA?! WHERE?!
SO...
* AHEM *
MOLLY TOLD ME YOU TWO ARE HAVING SOME "COMMUNICATION PROBLEM."
HUH? WHAT ARE YOU TALKING ABOUT, UNCLE FERRUS?
GO ON AND GET IT OUT. STATIC BETWEEN YOU TWO IS THE LAST THING I'LL NEED AT THIS PLACE.
WELL, I...
I DON'T THINK MY ROLE IN THIS TEAM IS APPRECIATED ENOUGH.
RO-BRO...? WHERE'S THIS COMING FROM? IS THIS ABOUT THE QUARRY?
LOOK AT THAT. THE HEALING'S BEGUN.
NOW, WE'VE GOT A GOOD HALF HOUR AHEAD OF US...
JUST ENOUGH TIME FOR A "VERY SPECIAL EPISODE" WHERE YOU, MAX AND STEEL, BURY THE HATCHET, PATCH THE FENCE AND GET BACK TO BEING A UNIT. GOT ME?
GOT ME?

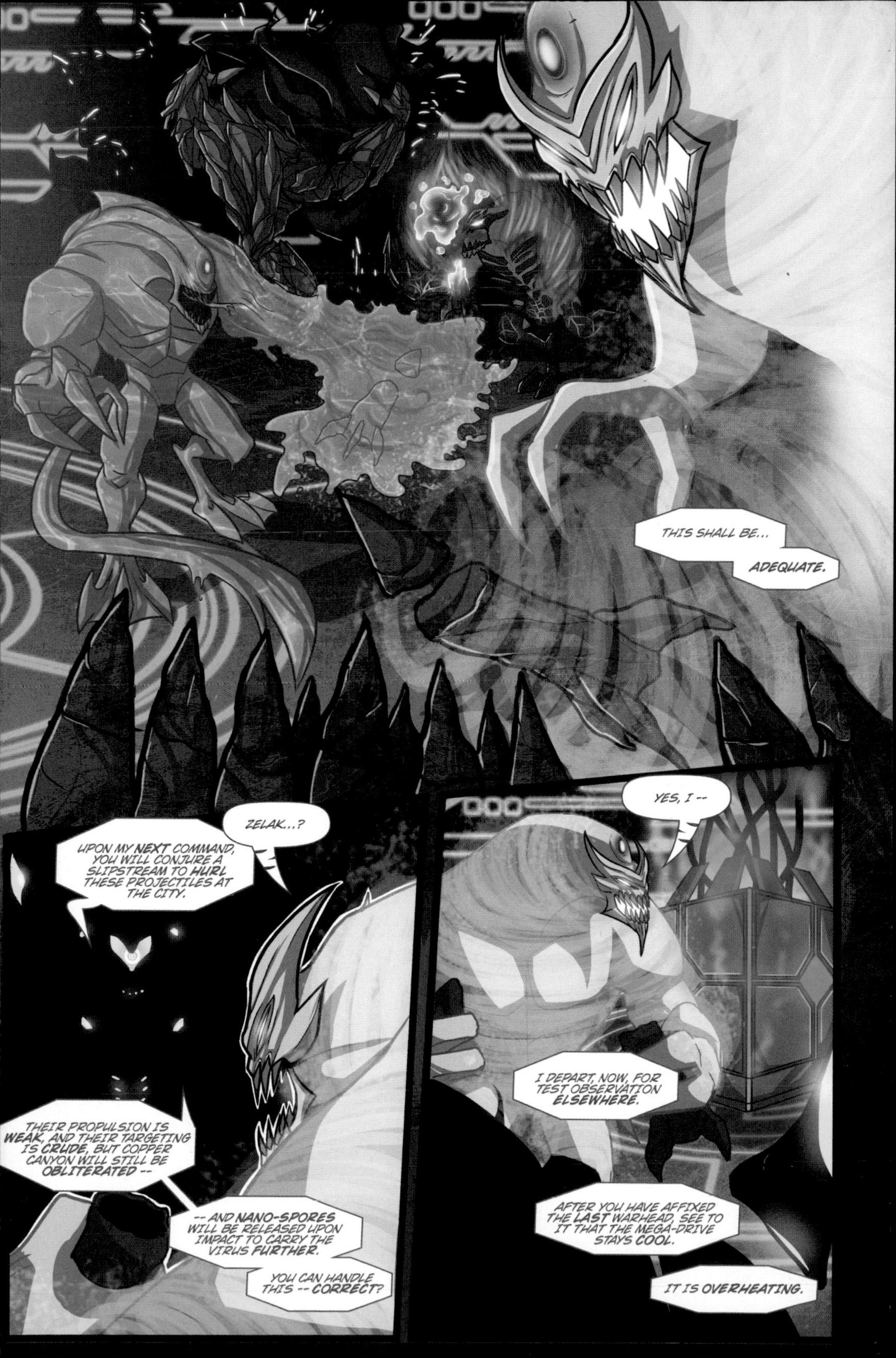
THIS SHALL BE... ADEQUATE.
ZELAK...?
UPON MY NEXT COMMAND, YOU WILL CONJURE A SLIPSTREAM TO HURL THESE PROJECTILES AT THE CITY.
THEIR PROPULSION IS WEAK, AND THEIR TARGETING IS CRUDE, BUT COPPER CANYON WILL STILL BE OBLITERATED --
-- AND NANO-SPORES WILL BE RELEASED UPON IMPACT TO CARRY THE VIRUS FURTHER.
YOU CAN HANDLE THIS -- CORRECT?
YES, I --
I DEPART, NOW, FOR TEST OBSERVATION ELSEWHERE.
AFTER YOU HAVE AFFIXED THE LAST WARHEAD, SEE TO IT THAT THE MEGA-DRIVE STAYS COOL.
IT IS OVERHEATING.

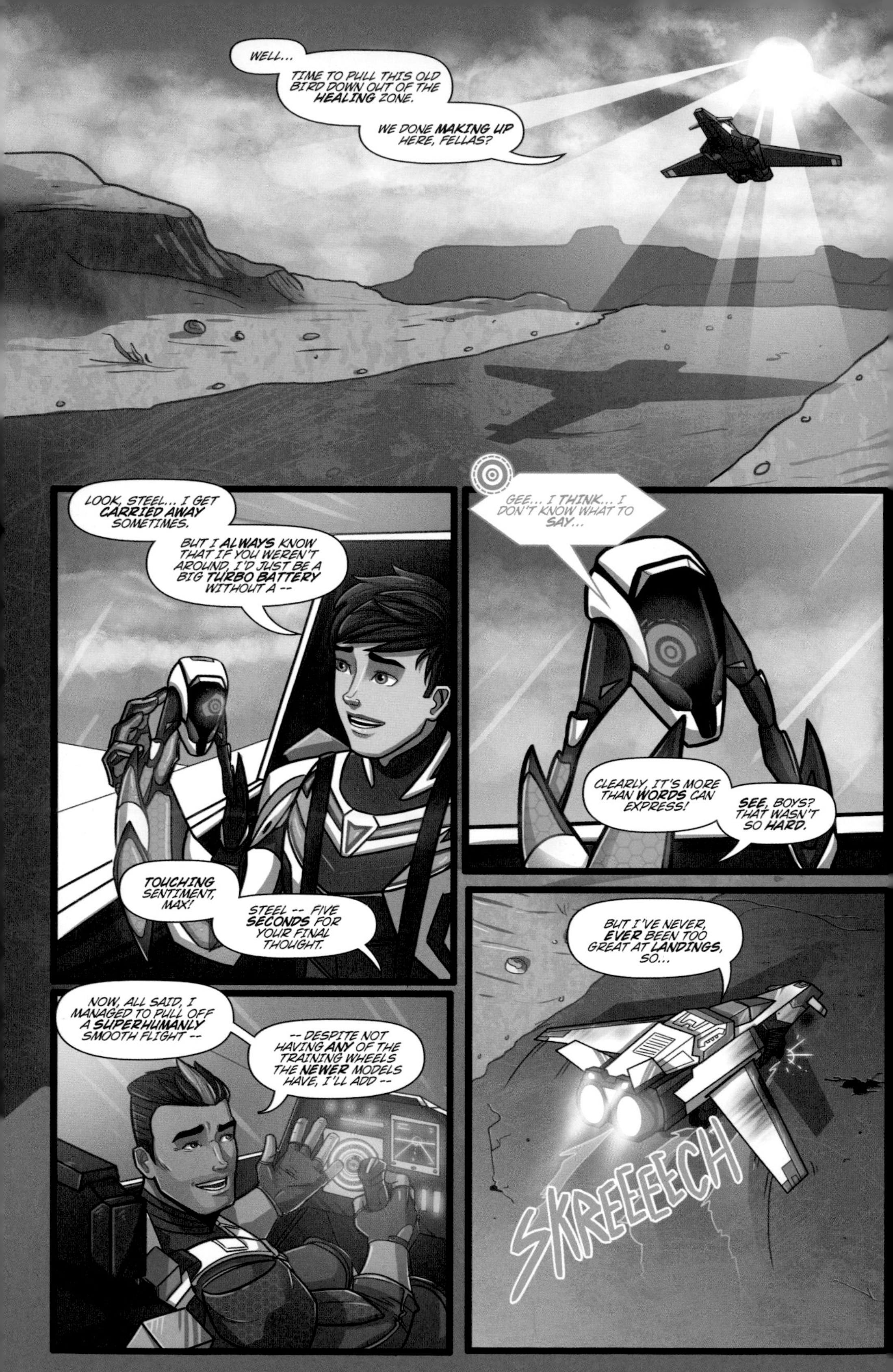
WELL...
TIME TO PULL THIS OLD BIRD DOWN OUT OF THE HEALING ZONE.
WE DONE MAKING UP HERE, FELLAS?
LOOK, STEEL... I GET CARRIED AWAY SOMETIMES.
BUT I ALWAYS KNOW THAT IF YOU WEREN'T AROUND, I'D JUST BE A BIG TURBO BATTERY WITHOUT A --
TOUCHING SENTIMENT, MAX!
STEEL -- FIVE SECONDS FOR YOUR FINAL THOUGHT.
GEE... I THINK... I DON'T KNOW WHAT TO SAY...
CLEARLY, IT'S MORE THAN WORDS CAN EXPRESS!
SEE, BOYS? THAT WASN'T SO HARD.
NOW, ALL SAID, I MANAGED TO PULL OFF A SUPERHUMANLY SMOOTH FLIGHT --
-- DESPITE NOT HAVING ANY OF THE TRAINING WHEELS THE NEWER MODELS HAVE, I'LL ADD --
BUT I'VE NEVER, EVER BEEN TOO GREAT AT LANDINGS, SO...
SKREEEECH

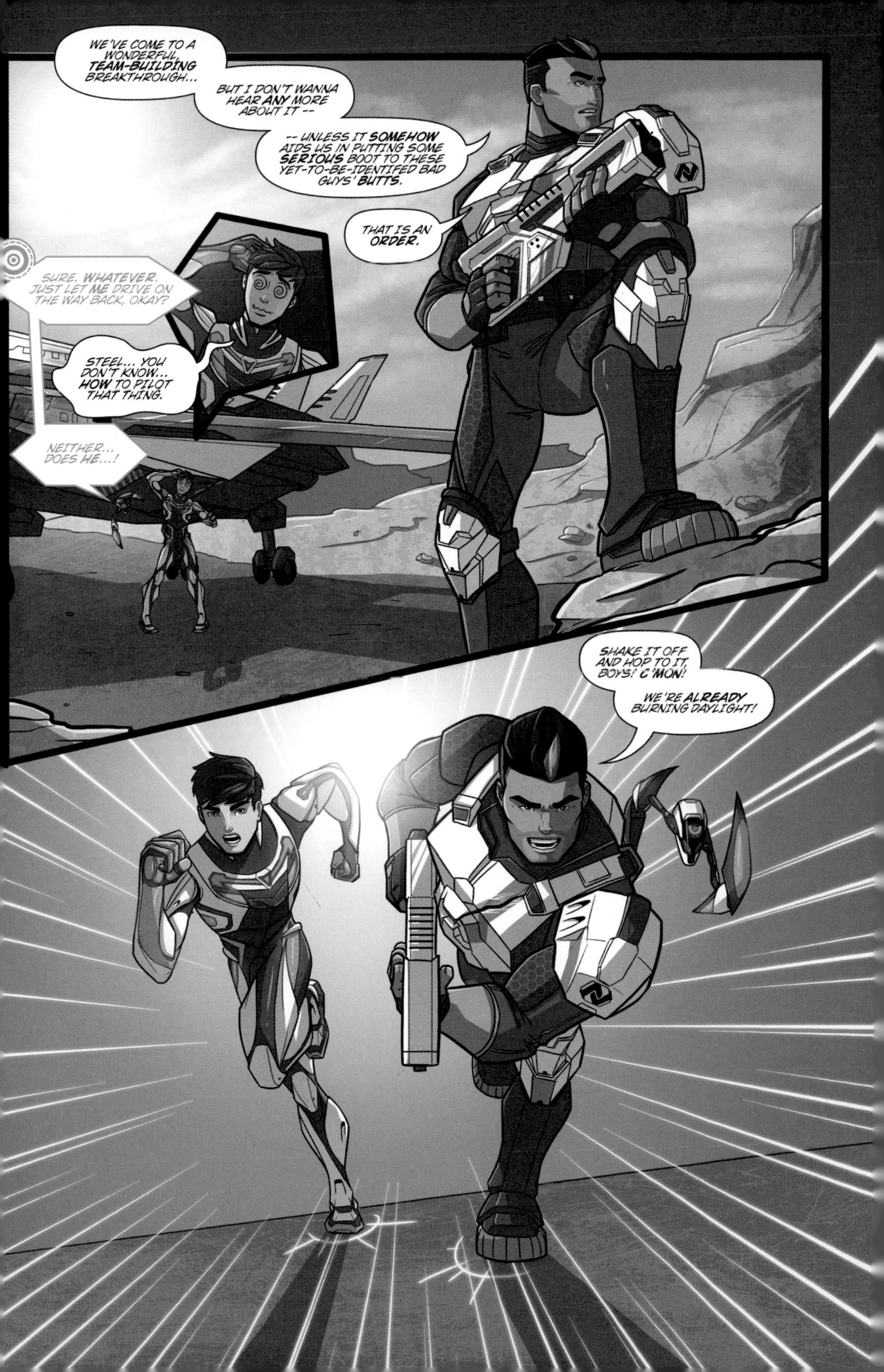
WE'VE COME TO A WONDERFUL, TEAM-BUILDING BREAKTHROUGH...
BUT I DON'T WANNA HEAR ANY MORE ABOUT IT --
-- UNLESS IT SOMEHOW AIDS US IN PUTTING SOME SERIOUS BOOT TO THESE YET-TO-BE-IDENTIFED BAD GUYS' BUTTS.
THAT IS AN ORDER.
SURE. WHATEVER. JUST LET ME DRIVE ON THE WAY BACK, OKAY?
STEEL... YOU DON'T KNOW... HOW TO PILOT THAT THING.
NEITHER... DOES HE...!
SHAKE IT OFF AND HOP TO IT, BOYS! C'MON!
WE'RE ALREADY BURNING DAYLIGHT!

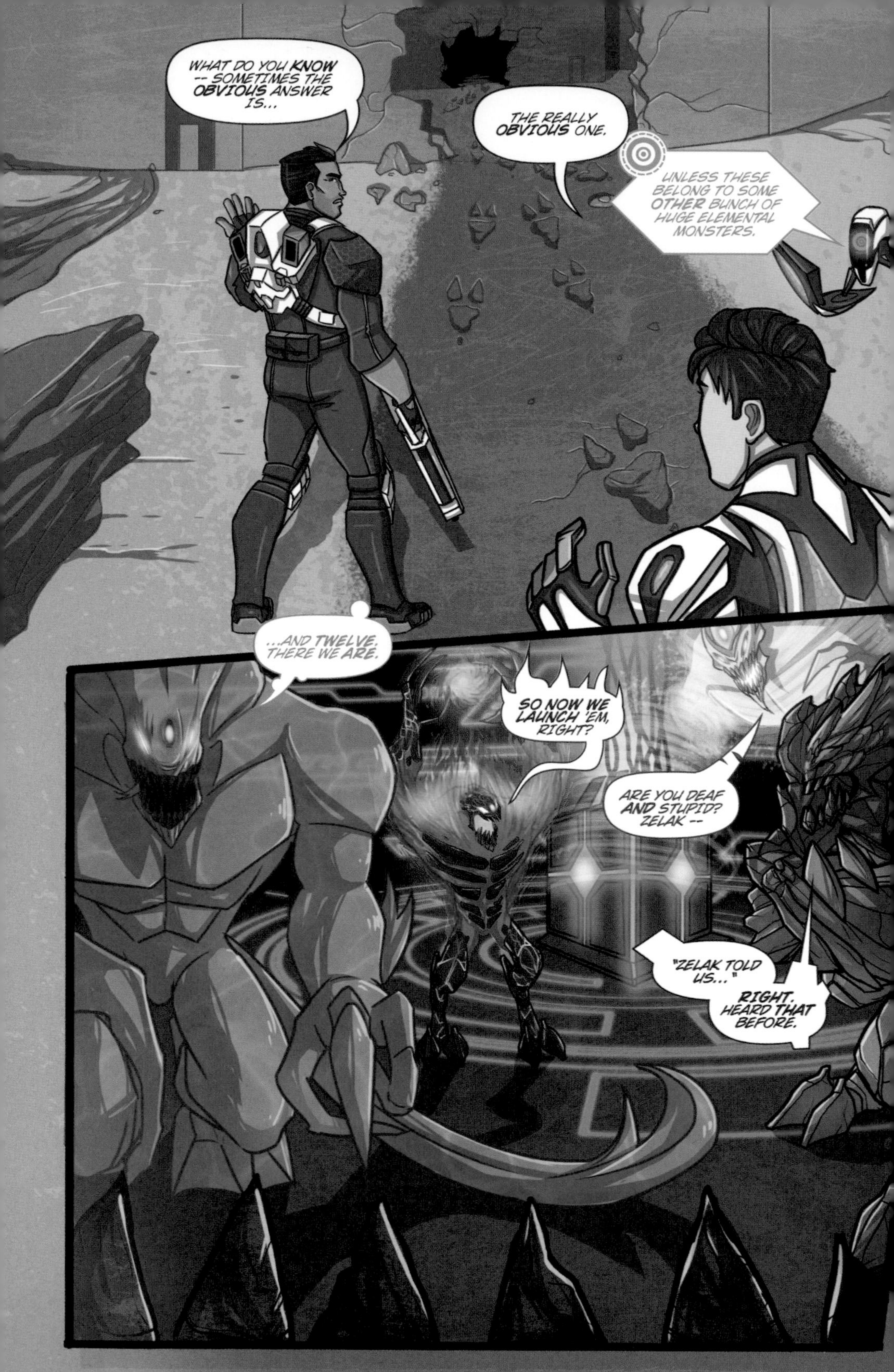
WHAT DO YOU KNOW -- SOMETIMES THE OBVIOUS ANSWER IS...
THE REALLY OBVIOUS ONE.
UNLESS THESE BELONG TO SOME OTHER BUNCH OF HUGE ELEMENTAL MONSTERS.
...AND TWELVE. THERE WE ARE.
SO NOW WE LAUNCH 'EM, RIGHT?
ARE YOU DEAF AND STUPID? ZELAK --
"ZELAK TOLD US..."
RIGHT. HEARD THAT BEFORE.

CHAPTER 4: DEBUG BY DAWN

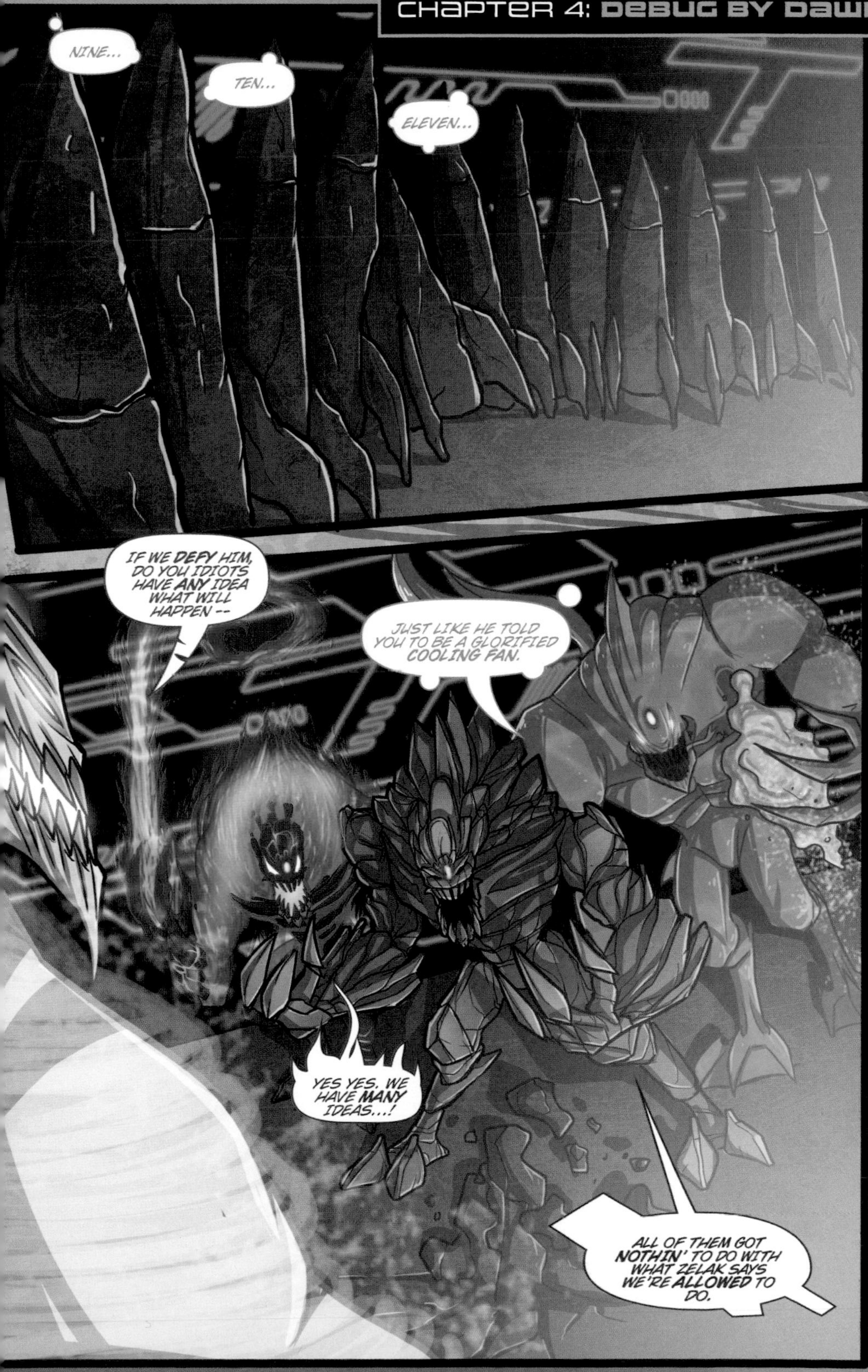
NINE...
TEN...
ELEVEN...
IF WE DEFY HIM, DO YOU IDIOTS HAVE ANY IDEA WHAT WILL HAPPEN --
JUST LIKE HE TOLD YOU TO BE A GLORIFIED COOLING FAN.
YES YES. WE HAVE MANY IDEAS...!
ALL OF THEM GOT NOTHIN' TO DO WITH WHAT ZELAK SAYS WE'RE ALLOWED TO DO.

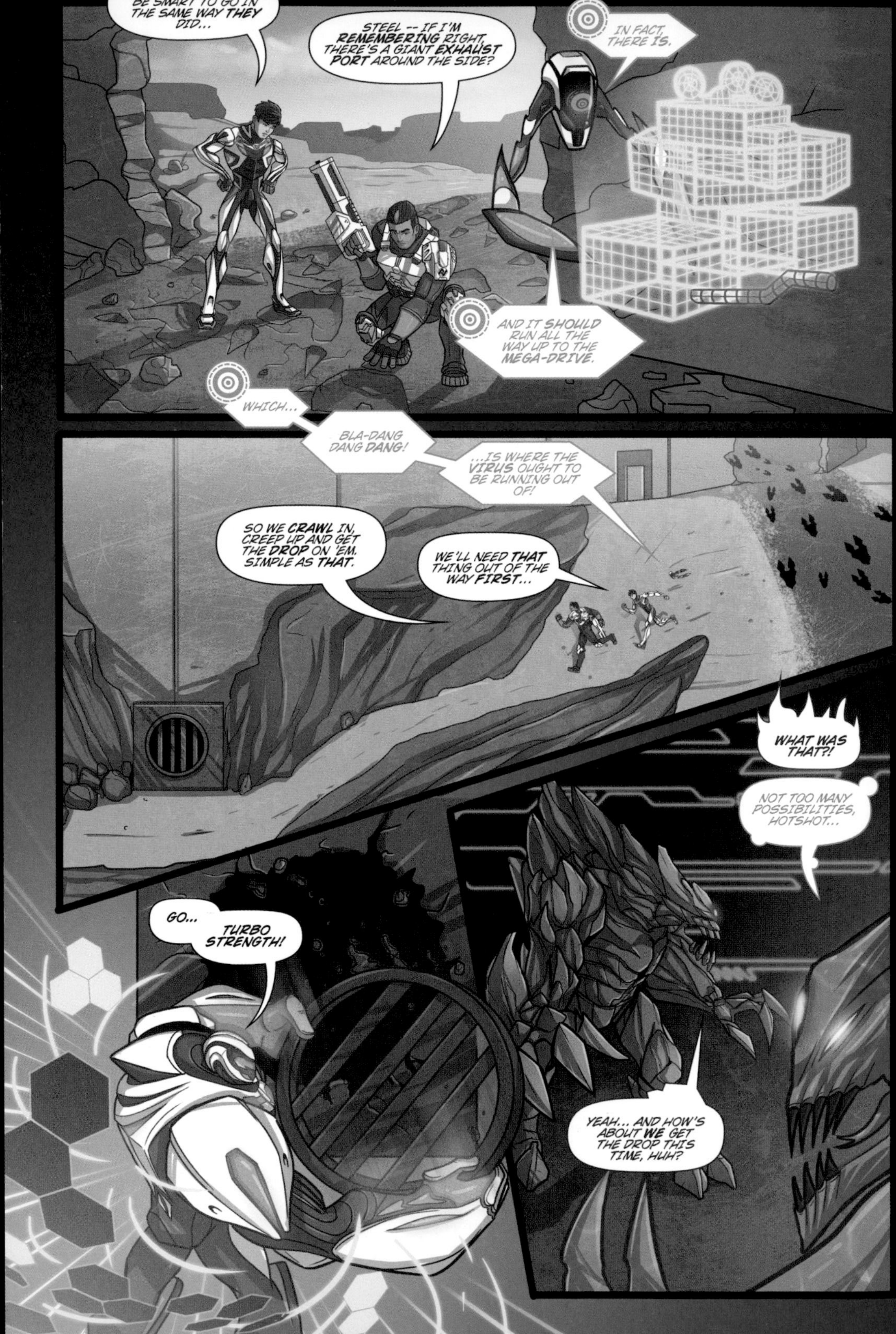
PROBABLY WOULDN'T BE SMART TO GO IN THE SAME WAY THEY DID...
STEEL -- IF I'M REMEMBERING RIGHT, THERE'S A GIANT EXHAUST PORT AROUND THE SIDE?
IN FACT, THERE IS.
AND IT SHOULD RUN ALL THE WAY UP TO THE MEGA-DRIVE.
WHICH...
BLA-DANG DANG DANG!
...IS WHERE THE VIRUS OUGHT TO BE RUNNING OUT OF!
SO WE CRAWL IN, CREEP UP AND GET THE DROP ON 'EM. SIMPLE AS THAT.
WE'LL NEED THAT THING OUT OF THE WAY FIRST...
WHAT WAS THAT?!
NOT TOO MANY POSSIBILITIES, HOTSHOT...
GO... TURBO STRENGTH!
YEAH... AND HOW'S ABOUT WE GET THE DROP THIS TIME, HUH?

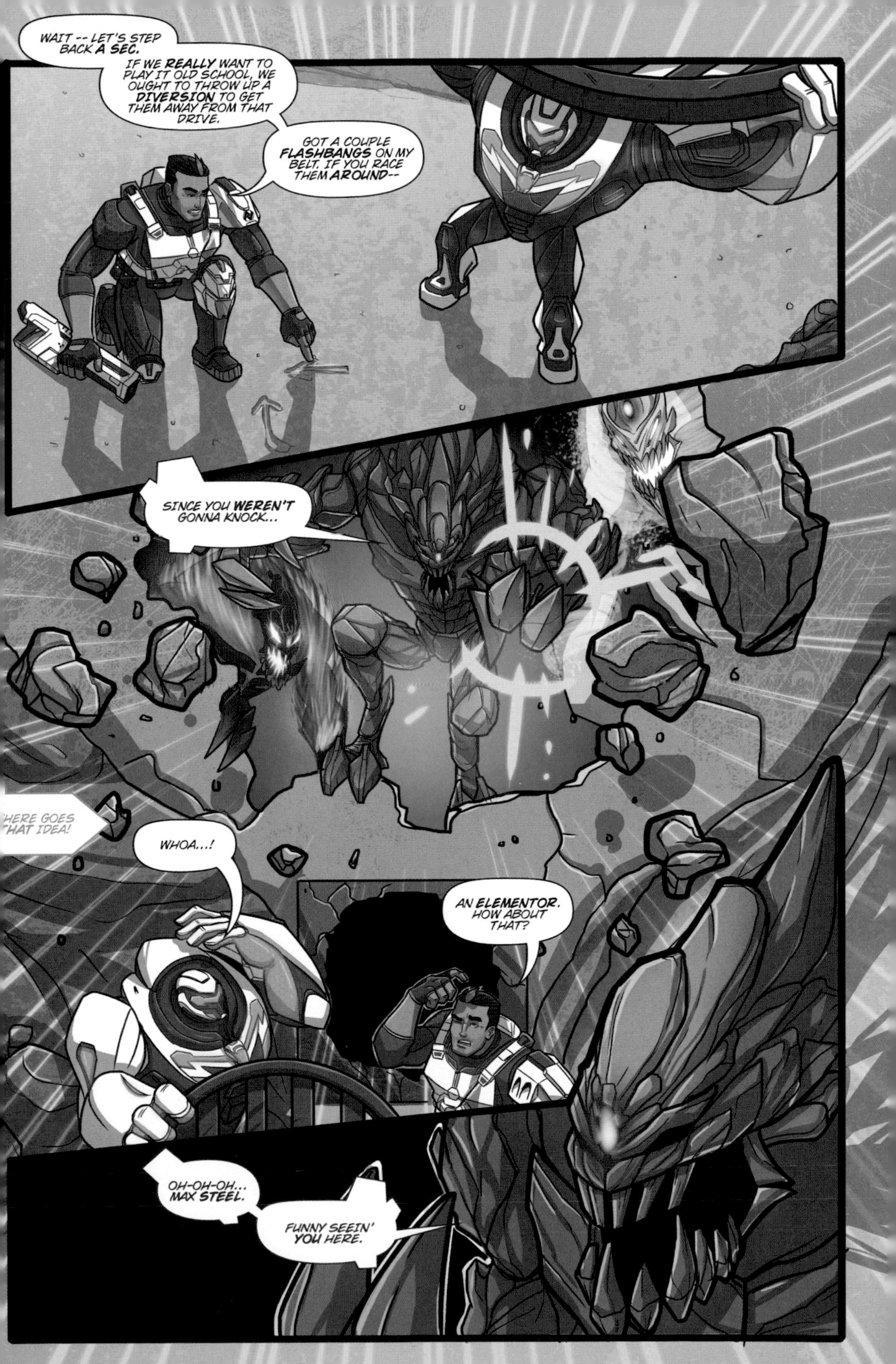
WAIT -- LET'S STEP BACK A SEC.
IF WE REALLY WANT TO PLAY IT OLD SCHOOL, WE OUGHT TO THROW UP A DIVERSION TO GET THEM AWAY FROM THAT DRIVE.
GOT A COUPLE FLASHBANGS ON MY BELT. IF YOU RACE THEM AROUND--
SINCE YOU WEREN'T GONNA KNOCK...
HERE GOES THAT IDEA!
WHOA...!
AN ELEMENTOR. HOW ABOUT THAT?
OH-OH-OH... MAX STEEL.
FUNNY SEEIN' YOU HERE.

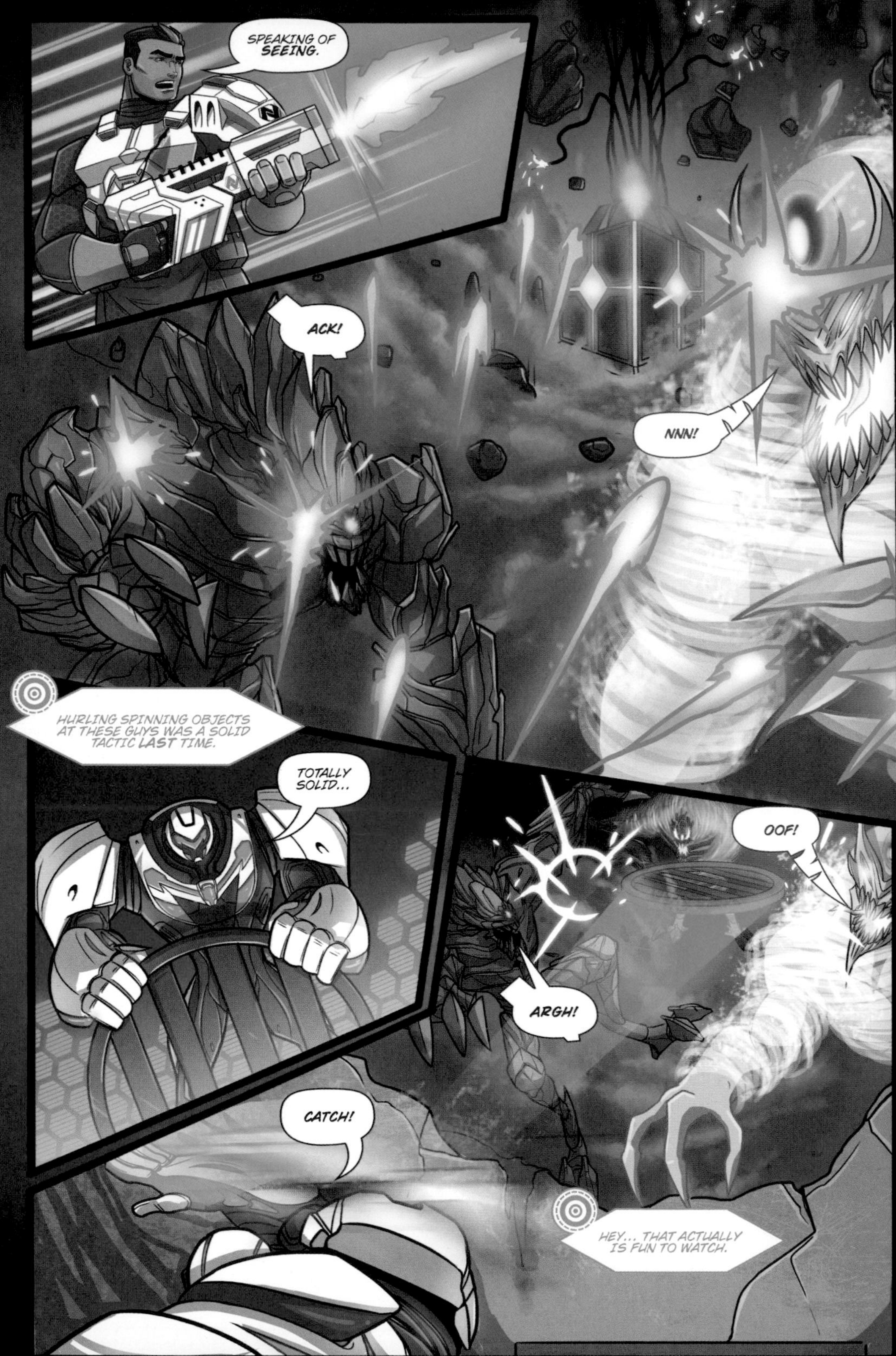
SPEAKING OF SEEING.
ACK!
NNN!
HURLING SPINNING OBJECTS AT THESE GUYS WAS A SOLID TACTIC LAST TIME.
TOTALLY SOLID...
OOF!
ARGH!
CATCH!
HEY... THAT ACTUALLY IS FUN TO WATCH.

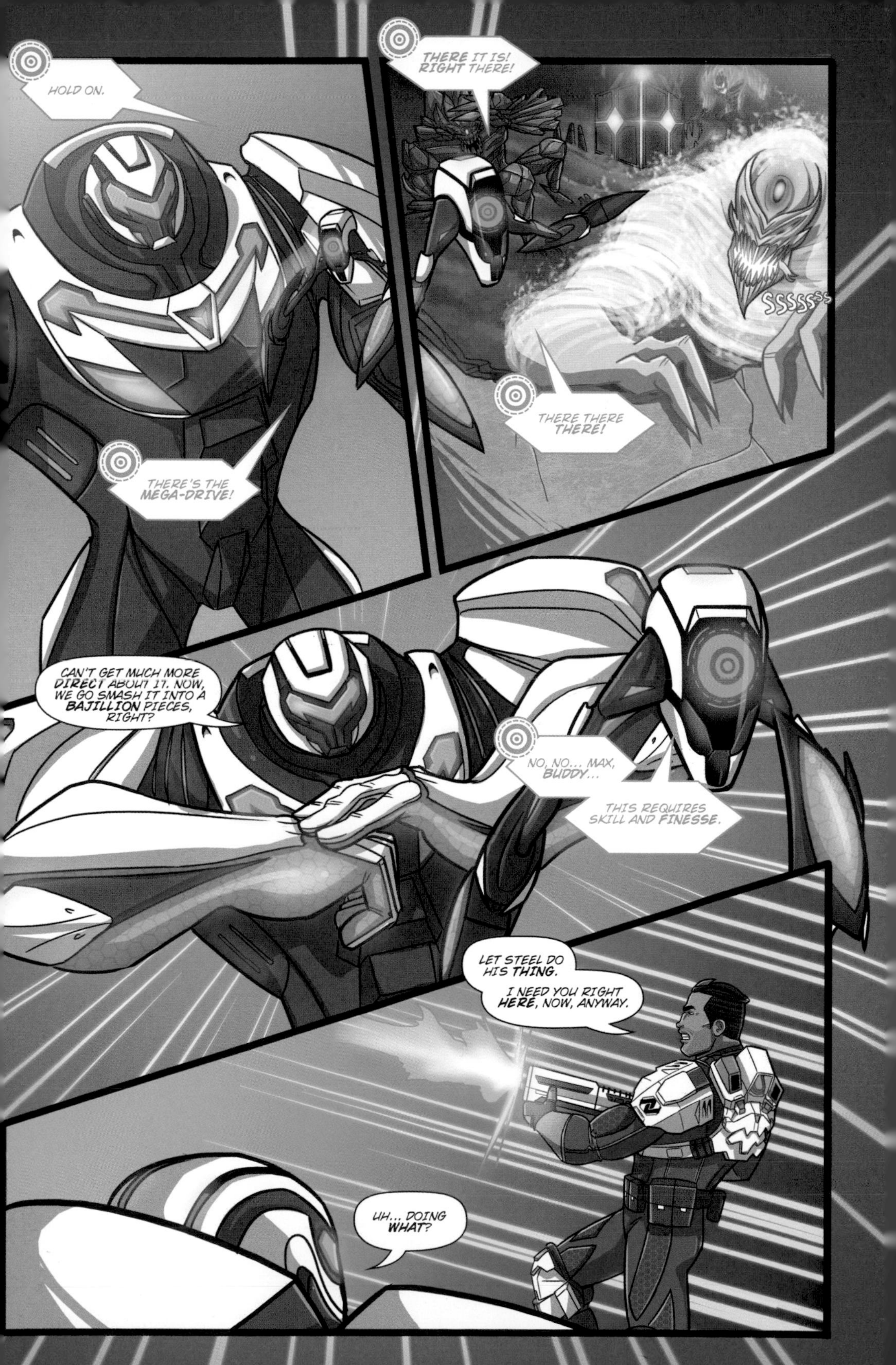
HOLD ON.
THERE'S THE MEGA-DRIVE!
THERE IT IS! RIGHT THERE!
SSSSSSS
THERE THERE THERE!
CAN'T GET MUCH MORE DIRECT ABOUT IT. NOW, WE GO SMASH IT INTO A BAJILLION PIECES, RIGHT?
NO, NO... MAX, BUDDY...
THIS REQUIRES SKILL AND FINESSE.
LET STEEL DO HIS THING.
I NEED YOU RIGHT HERE, NOW, ANYWAY.
UH... DOING WHAT?

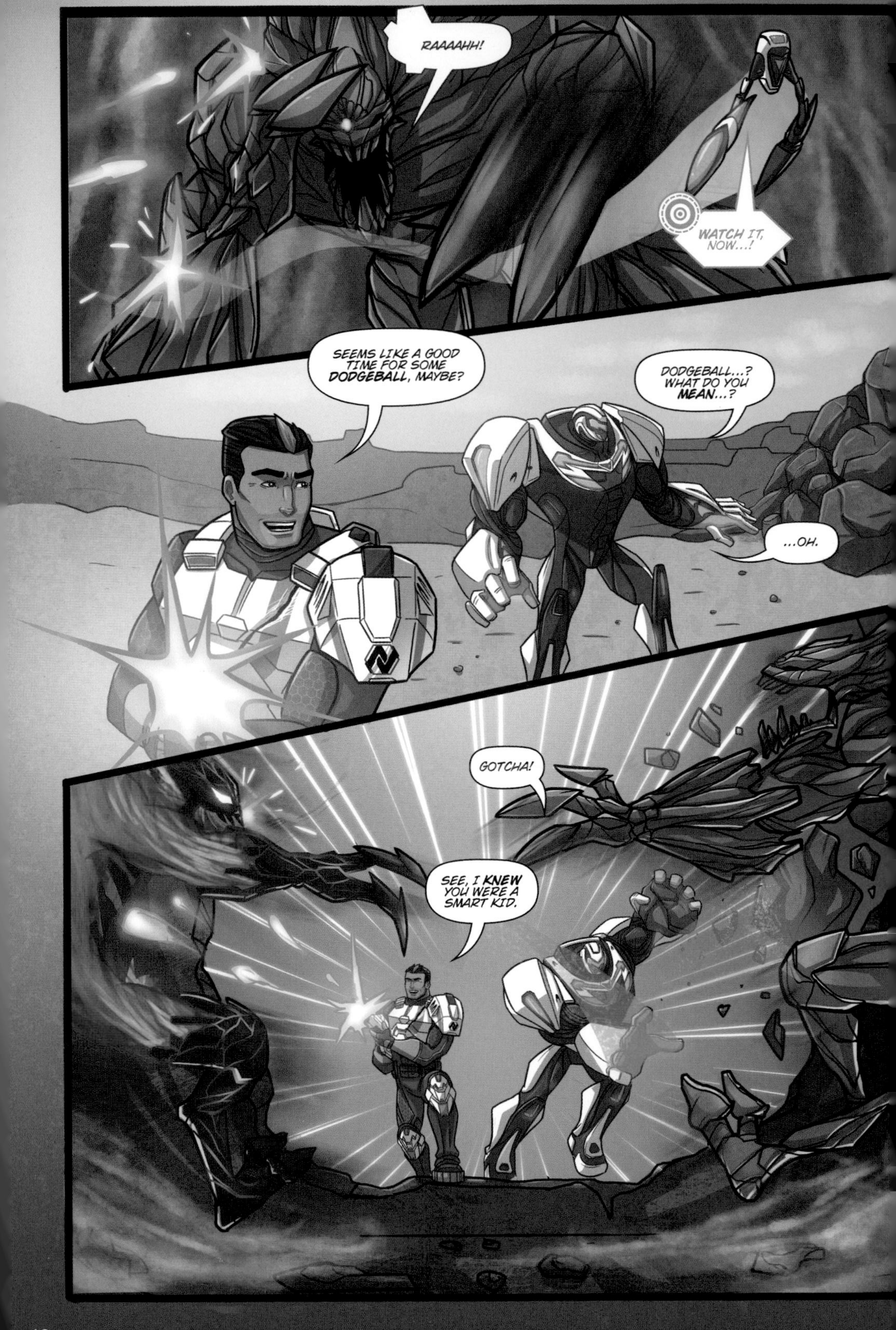
RAAAAHH!
WATCH IT, NOW...!
SEEMS LIKE A GOOD TIME FOR SOME DODGEBALL, MAYBE?
DODGEBALL...? WHAT DO YOU MEAN...?
...OH.
GOTCHA!
SEE, I KNEW YOU WERE A SMART KID.

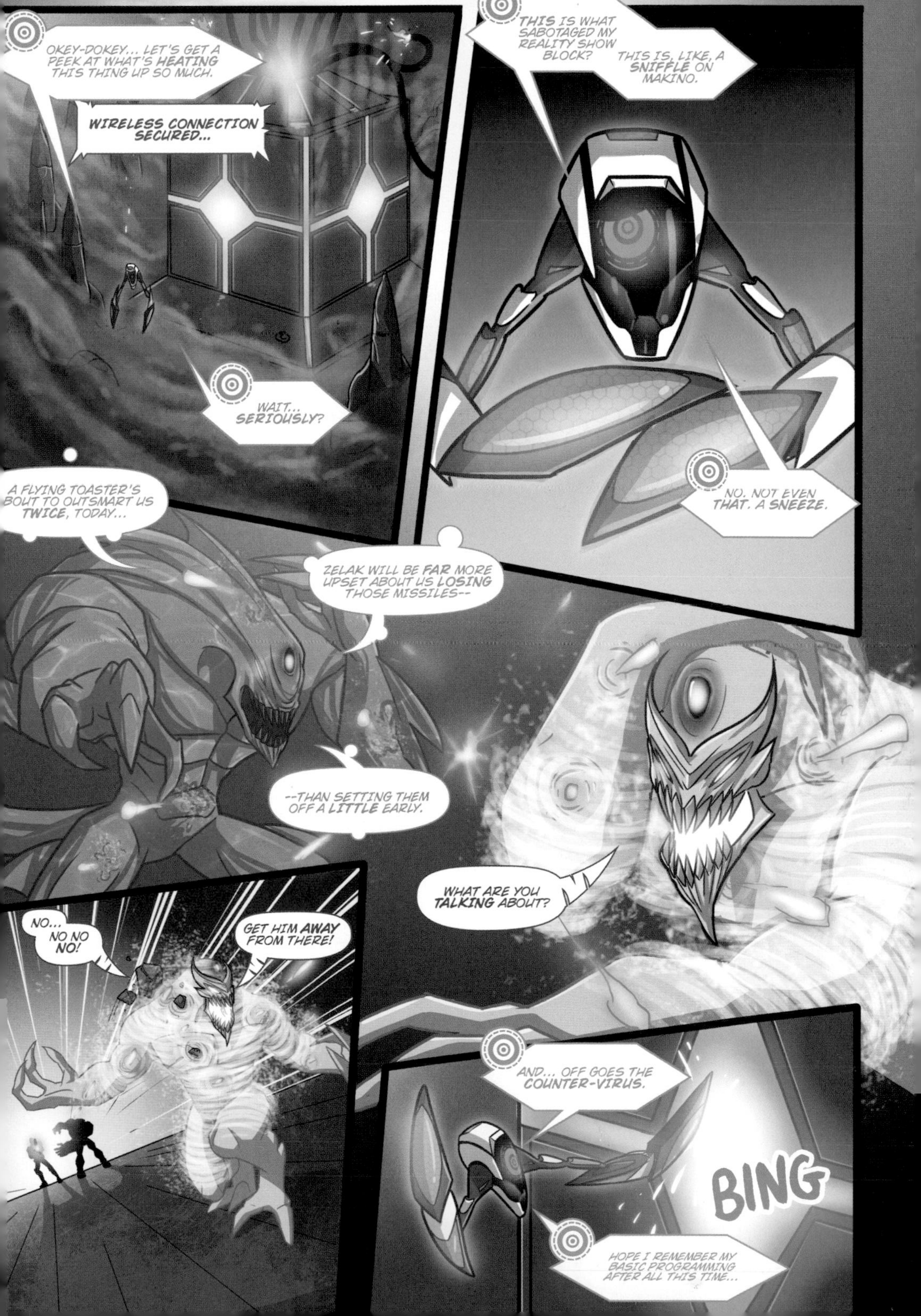

OKEY-DOKEY... LET'S GET A PEEK AT WHAT'S HEATING THIS THING UP SO MUCH.
WIRELESS CONNECTION SECURED...
WAIT... SERIOUSLY?
THIS IS WHAT SABOTAGED MY REALITY SHOW BLOCK?
THIS IS, LIKE, A SNIFFLE ON MAKINO.
NO. NOT EVEN THAT. A SNEEZE.
A FLYING TOASTER'S 'BOUT TO OUTSMART US TWICE, TODAY...
ZELAK WILL BE FAR MORE UPSET ABOUT US LOSING THOSE MISSILES--
--THAN SETTING THEM OFF A LITTLE EARLY.
WHAT ARE YOU TALKING ABOUT?
NO... NO NO NO!
GET HIM AWAY FROM THERE!
AND... OFF GOES THE COUNTER-VIRUS.
BING
HOPE I REMEMBER MY BASIC PROGRAMMING AFTER ALL THIS TIME...

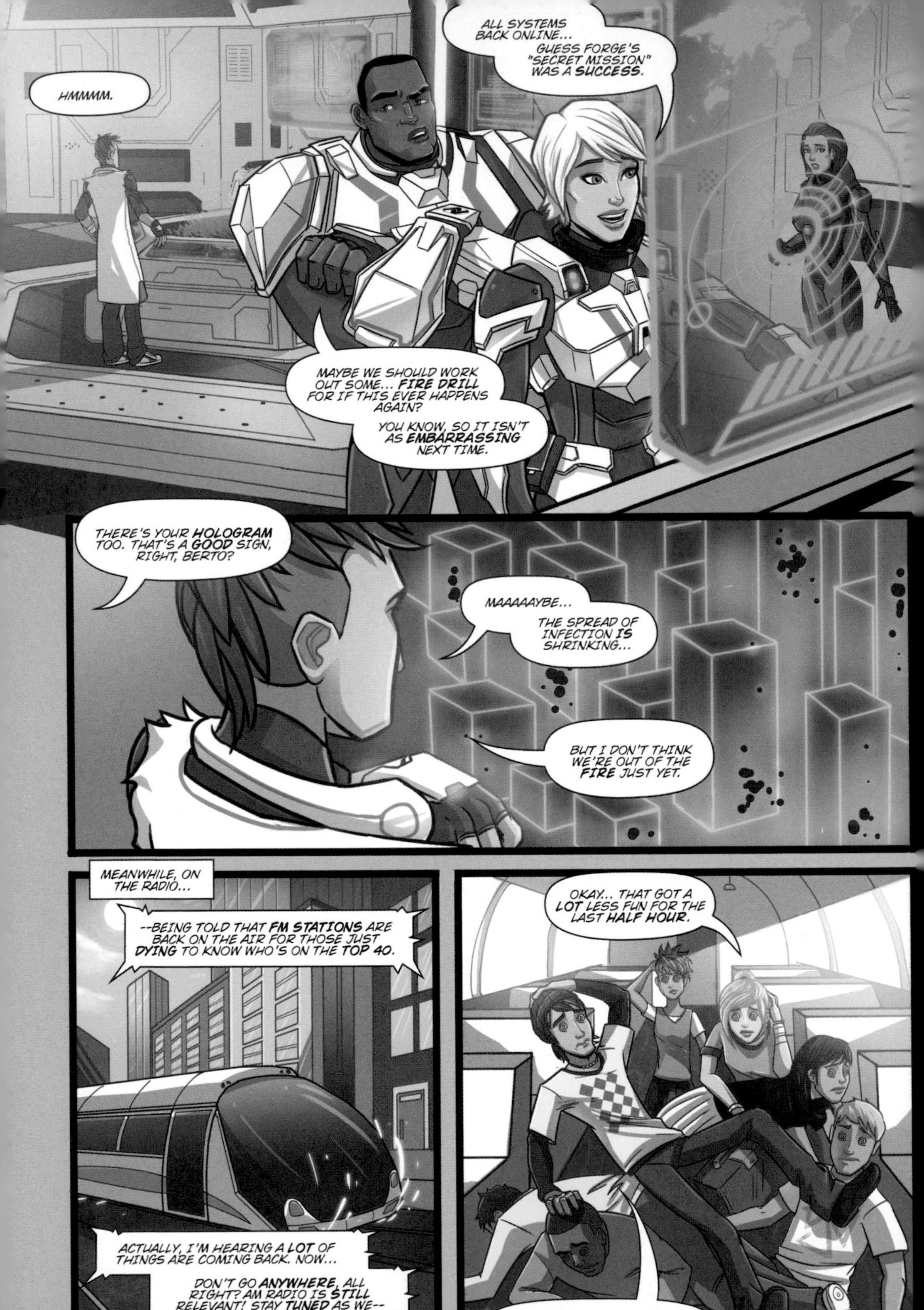
HMMMM.
ALL SYSTEMS BACK ONLINE...
GUESS FORGE'S "SECRET MISSION" WAS A SUCCESS.
MAYBE WE SHOULD WORK OUT SOME... FIRE DRILL FOR IF THIS EVER HAPPENS AGAIN?
YOU KNOW, SO IT ISN'T AS EMBARRASSING NEXT TIME.
THERE'S YOUR HOLOGRAM TOO. THAT'S A GOOD SIGN, RIGHT, BERTO?
MAAAAAYBE...
THE SPREAD OF INFECTION IS SHRINKING...
BUT I DON'T THINK WE'RE OUT OF THE FIRE JUST YET.
MEANWHILE, ON THE RADIO...
--BEING TOLD THAT FM STATIONS ARE BACK ON THE AIR FOR THOSE JUST DYING TO KNOW WHO'S ON THE TOP 40.
ACTUALLY, I'M HEARING A LOT OF THINGS ARE COMING BACK. NOW...
DON'T GO ANYWHERE, ALL RIGHT? AM RADIO IS STILL RELEVANT! STAY TUNED AS WE--
OKAY... THAT GOT A LOT LESS FUN FOR THE LAST HALF HOUR.
I THINK MY STOMACH'S STILL FLOATING SOMEWHERE BACK AT THE 3RD ST. STOP.

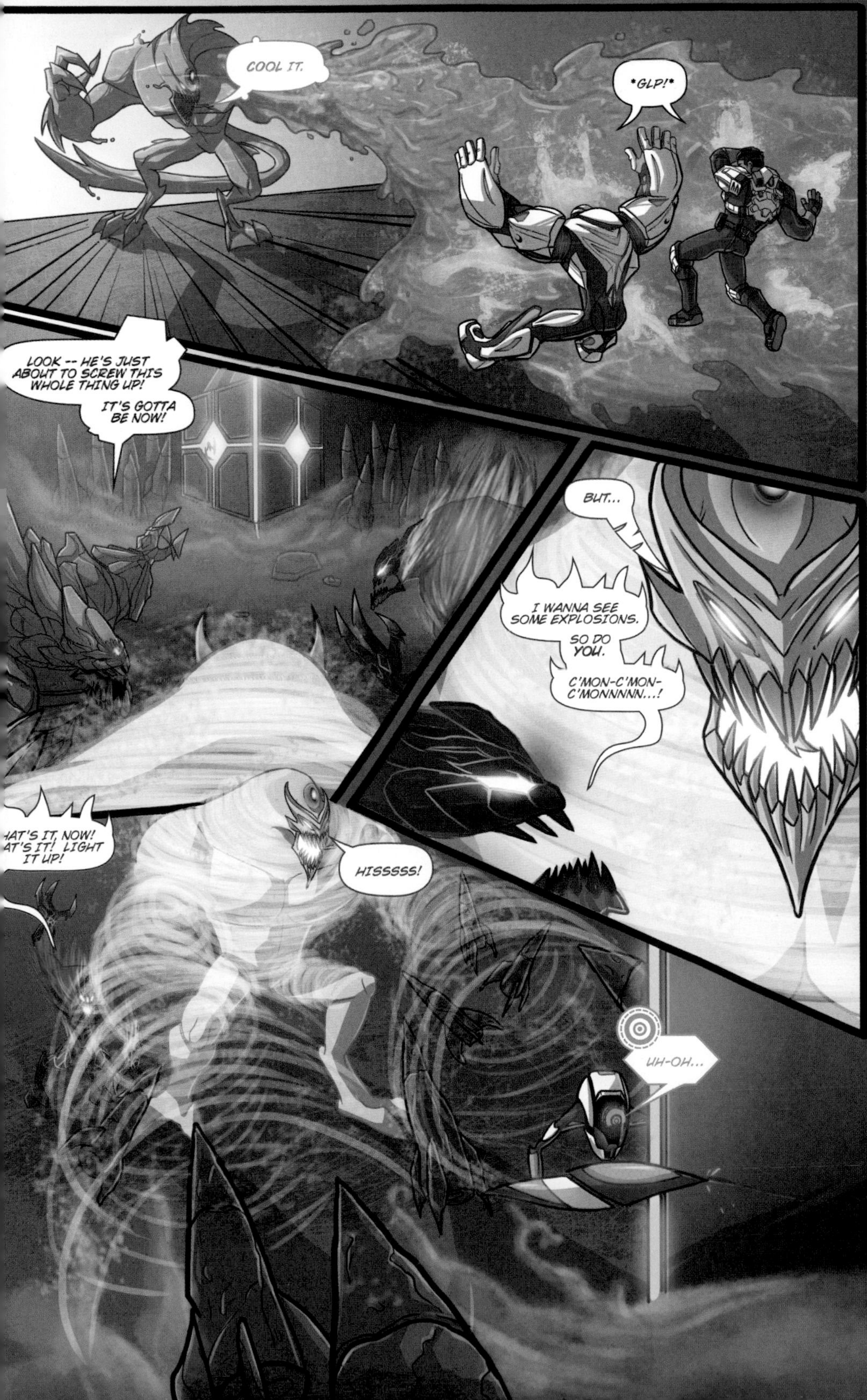
COOL IT.
GLP!
LOOK -- HE'S JUST ABOUT TO SCREW THIS WHOLE THING UP!
IT'S GOTTA BE NOW!
BUT...
I WANNA SEE SOME EXPLOSIONS.
SO DO YOU.
C'MON-C'MON-C'MONNNNN...!
HISSSSS!
UH-OH...

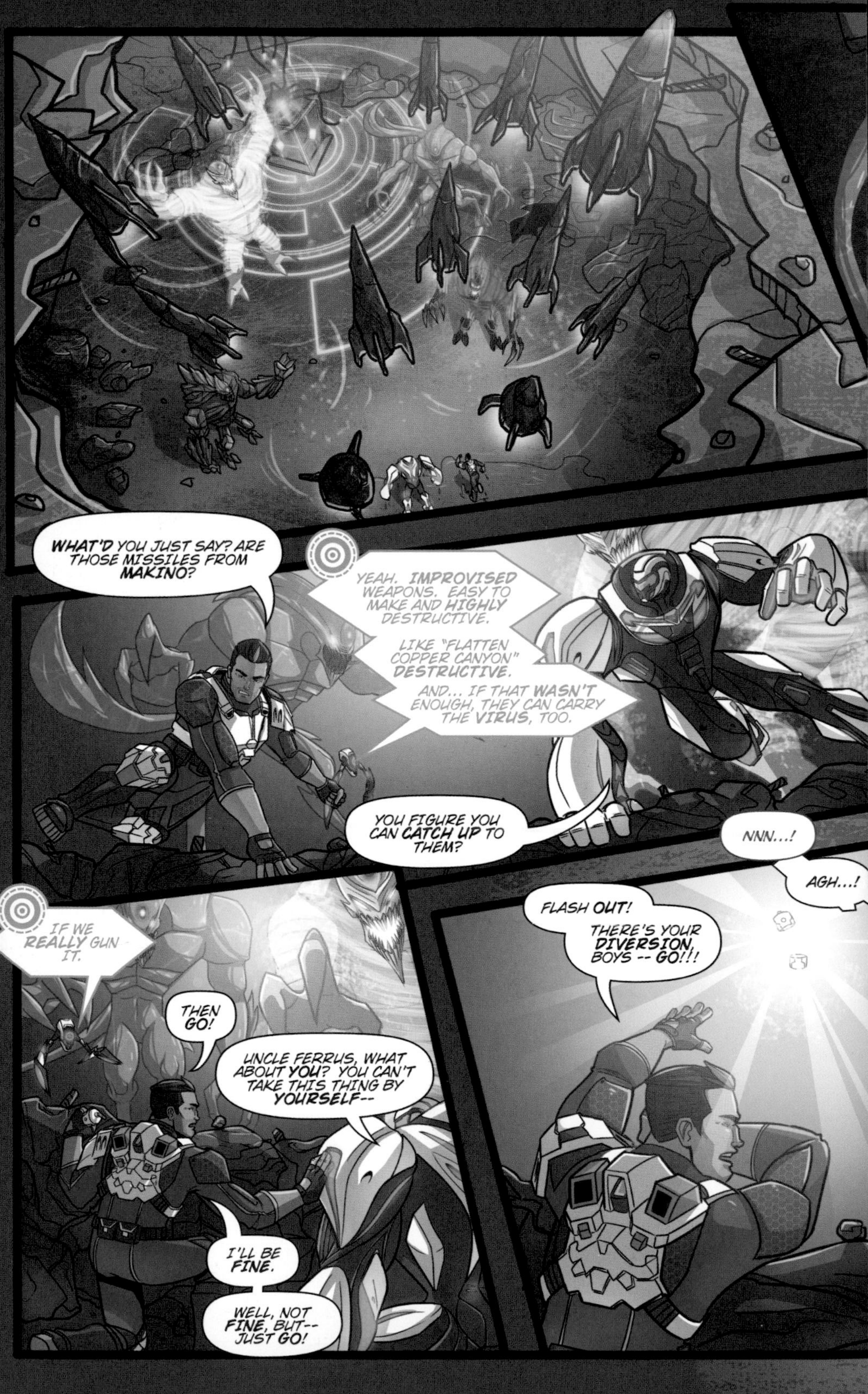
WHAT'D YOU JUST SAY? ARE THOSE MISSILES FROM MAKINO?
YEAH. IMPROVISED WEAPONS. EASY TO MAKE AND HIGHLY DESTRUCTIVE.
LIKE "FLATTEN COPPER CANYON" DESTRUCTIVE.
AND... IF THAT WASN'T ENOUGH, THEY CAN CARRY THE VIRUS, TOO.
YOU FIGURE YOU CAN CATCH UP TO THEM?
IF WE REALLY GUN IT.
THEN GO!
UNCLE FERRUS, WHAT ABOUT YOU? YOU CAN'T TAKE THIS THING BY YOURSELF--
I'LL BE FINE.
WELL, NOT FINE, BUT-- JUST GO!
NNN...!
AGH...!
FLASH OUT!
THERE'S YOUR DIVERSION, BOYS -- GO!!!

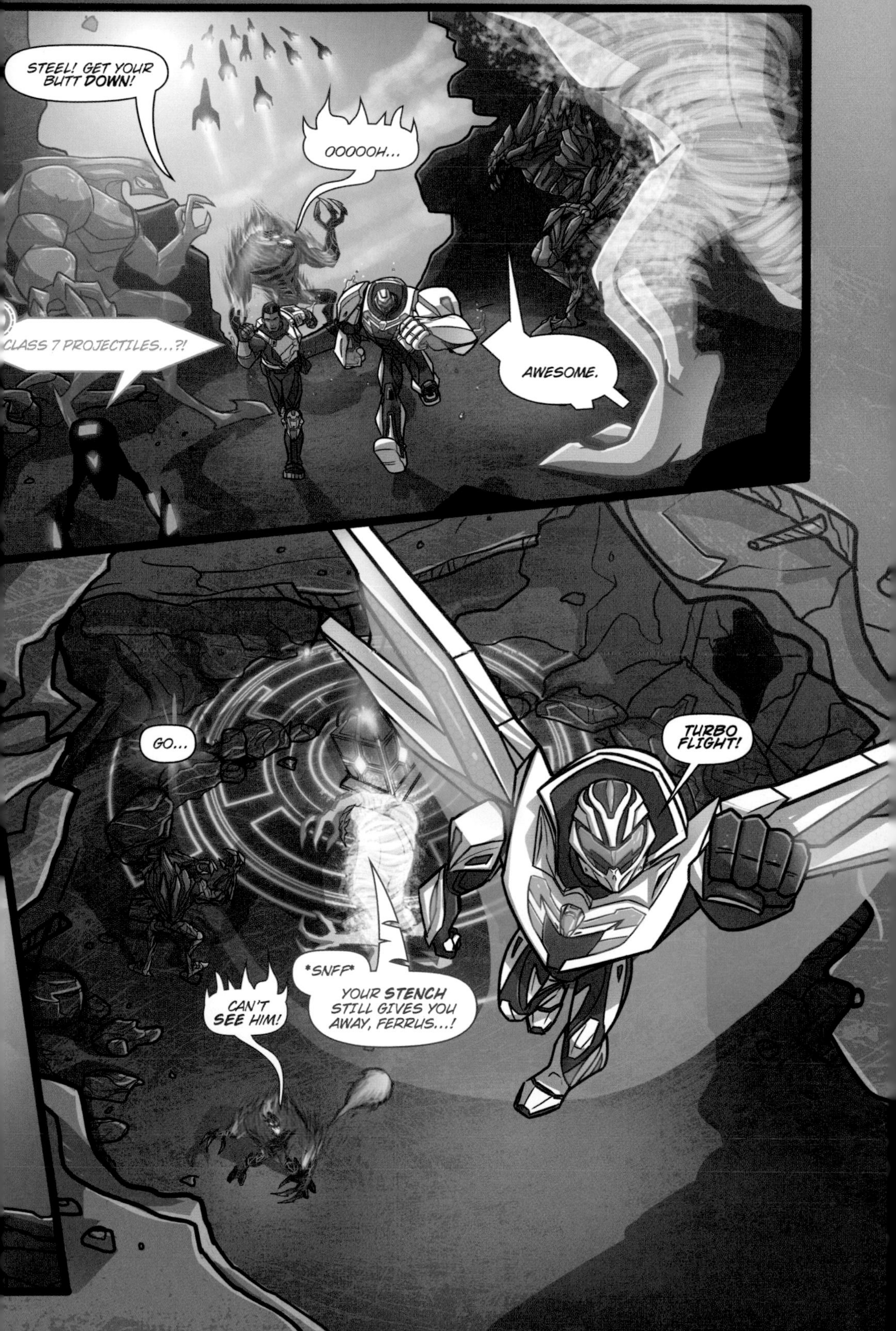
STEEL! GET YOUR BUTT DOWN!
OOOOOH...
CLASS 7 PROJECTILES...?!
AWESOME.
GO...
TURBO FLIGHT!
SNFF YOUR STENCH STILL GIVES YOU AWAY, FERRUS...!
CAN'T SEE HIM!

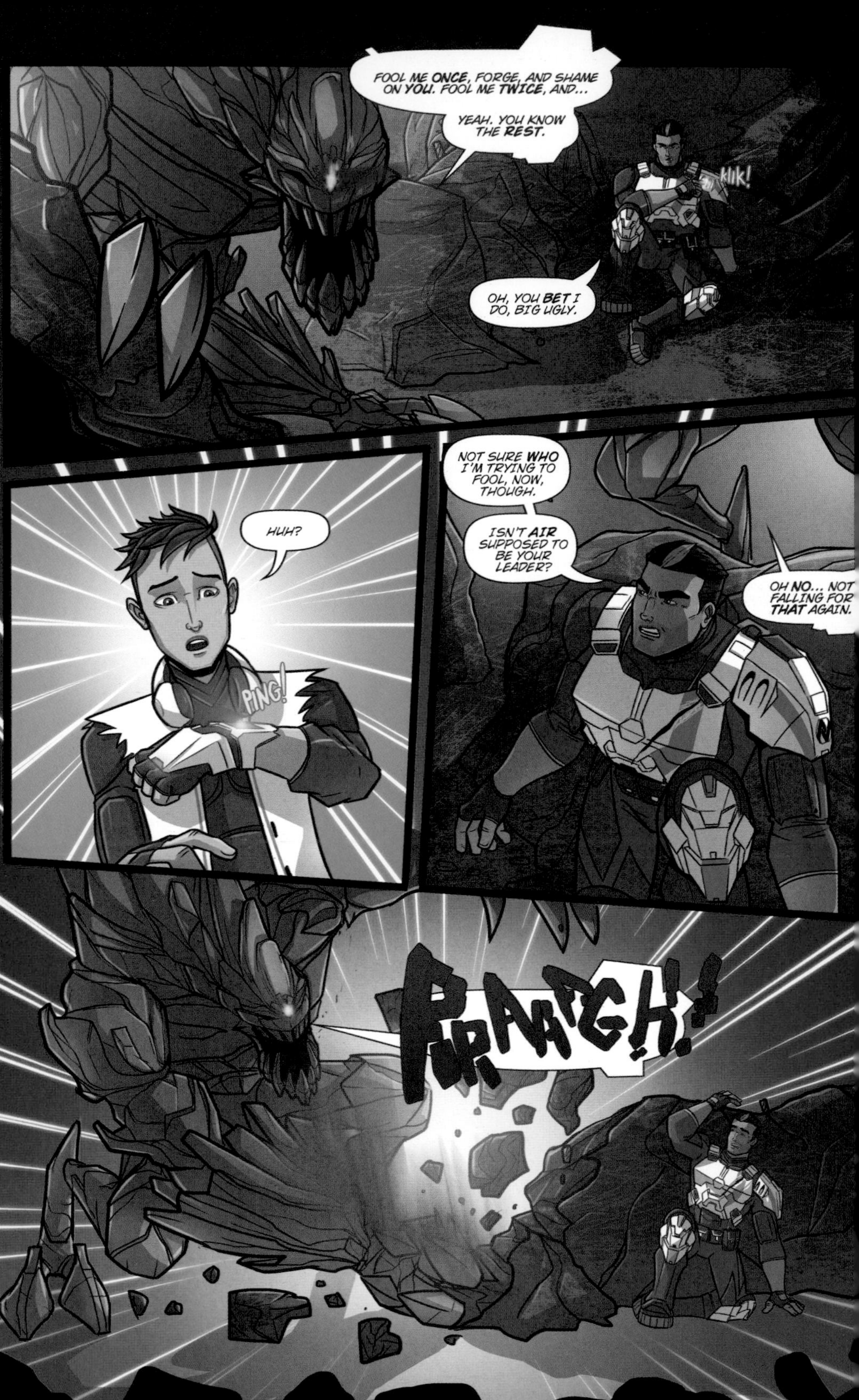

FOOL ME ONCE, FORGE, AND SHAME ON YOU. FOOL ME TWICE, AND...
YEAH. YOU KNOW THE REST.
KLIK!
OH, YOU BET I DO, BIG UGLY.
HUH?
PING!
NOT SURE WHO I'M TRYING TO FOOL, NOW, THOUGH.
ISN'T AIR SUPPOSED TO BE YOUR LEADER?
OH NO... NOT FALLING FOR THAT AGAIN.
RRAAAGH!!

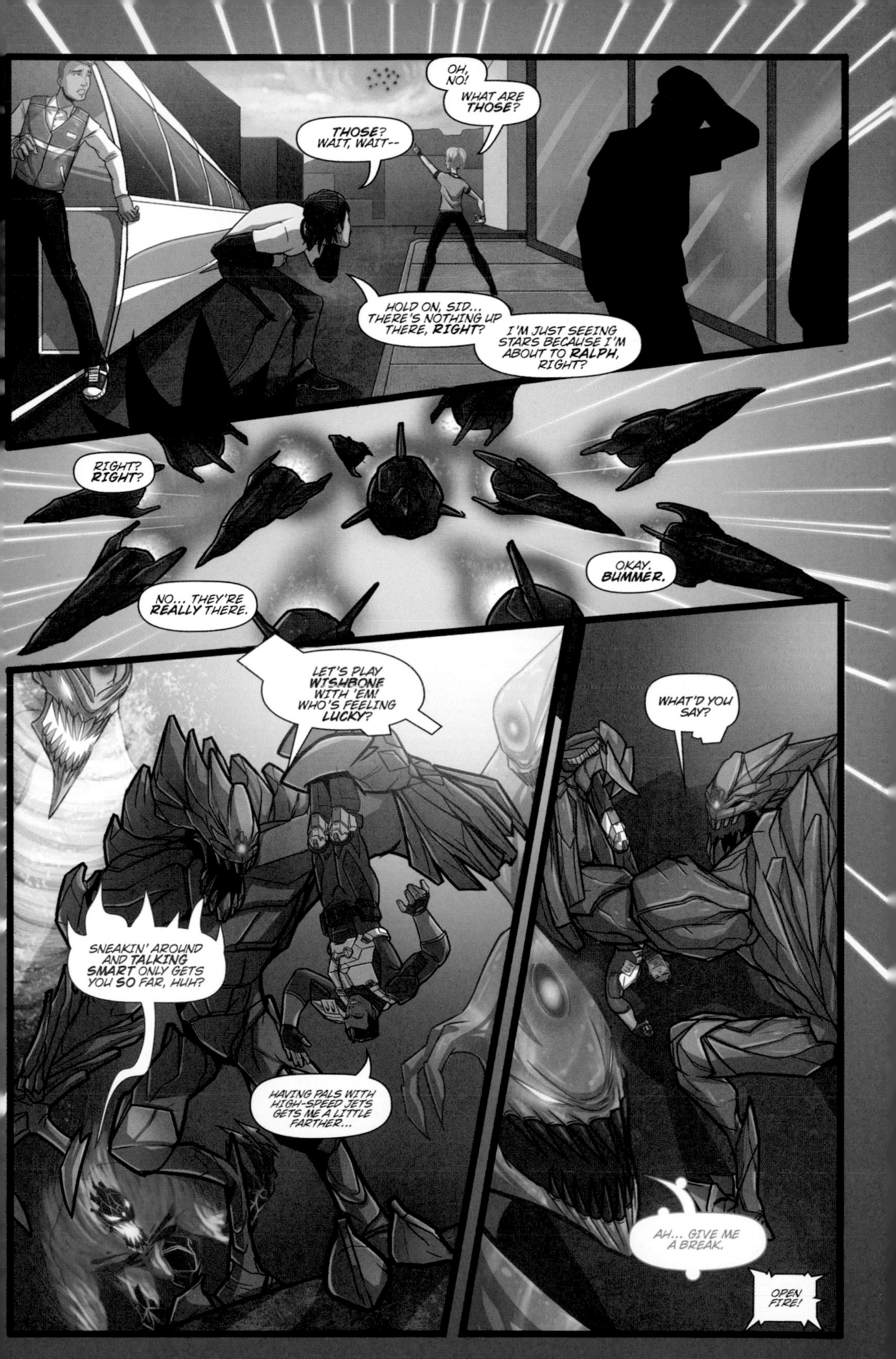
OH, NO!
WHAT ARE THOSE?
THOSE? WAIT, WAIT--
HOLD ON, SID... THERE'S NOTHING UP THERE, RIGHT?
I'M JUST SEEING STARS BECAUSE I'M ABOUT TO RALPH, RIGHT?
RIGHT? RIGHT?
OKAY. BUMMER.
NO... THEY'RE REALLY THERE.
LET'S PLAY WISHBONE WITH 'EM! WHO'S FEELING LUCKY?
SNEAKIN' AROUND AND TALKING SMART ONLY GETS YOU SO FAR, HUH?
HAVING PALS WITH HIGH-SPEED JETS GETS ME A LITTLE FARTHER...
WHAT'D YOU SAY?
AH... GIVE ME A BREAK.
OPEN FIRE!

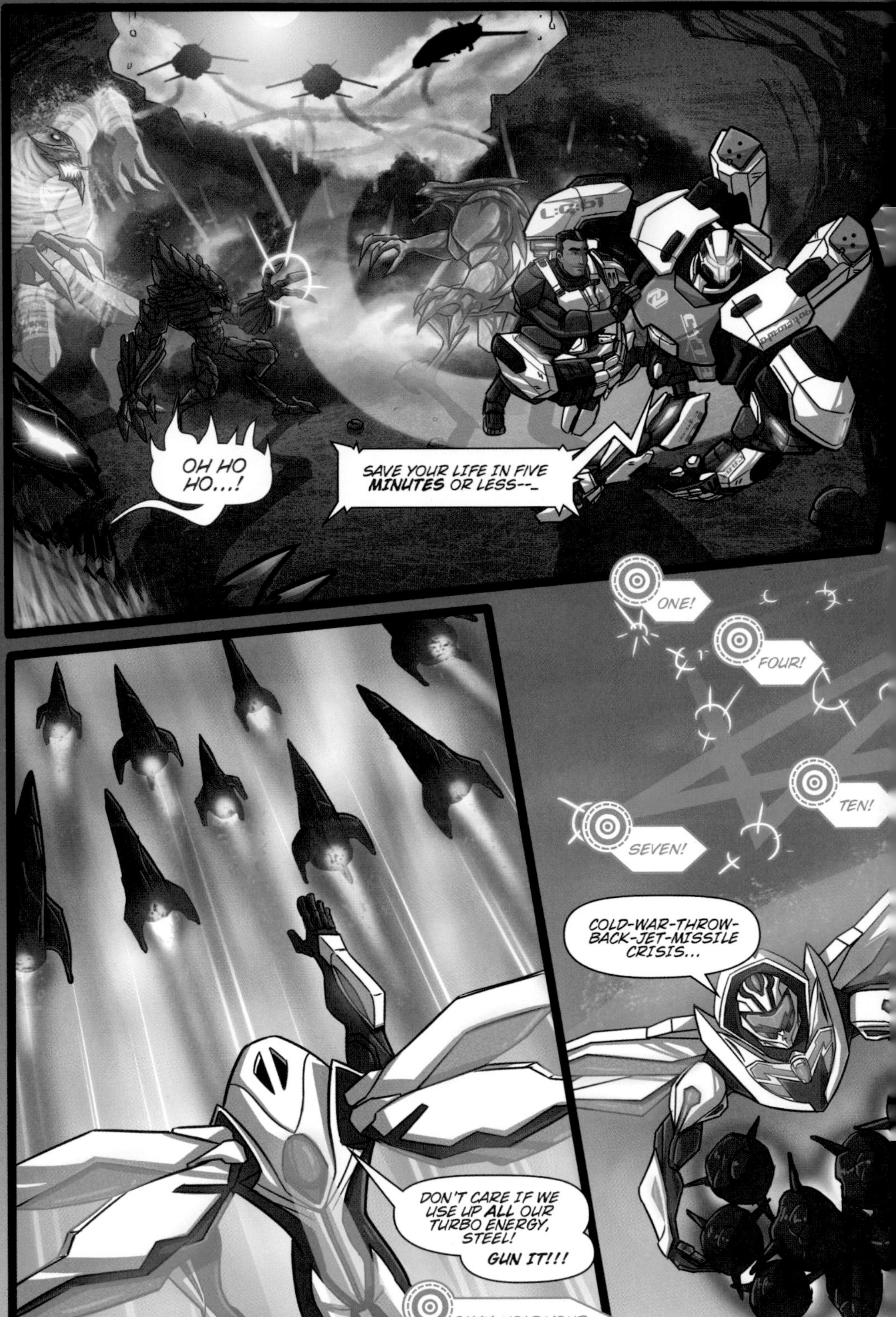

OH HO HO...!
SAVE YOUR LIFE IN FIVE MINUTES OR LESS--
ONE!
FOUR!
TEN!
SEVEN!
COLD-WAR-THROW-BACK-JET-MISSILE CRISIS...
DON'T CARE IF WE USE UP ALL OUR TURBO ENERGY, STEEL!
GUN IT!!!
OKAY. HOLD YOUR BREATH, NOW...!

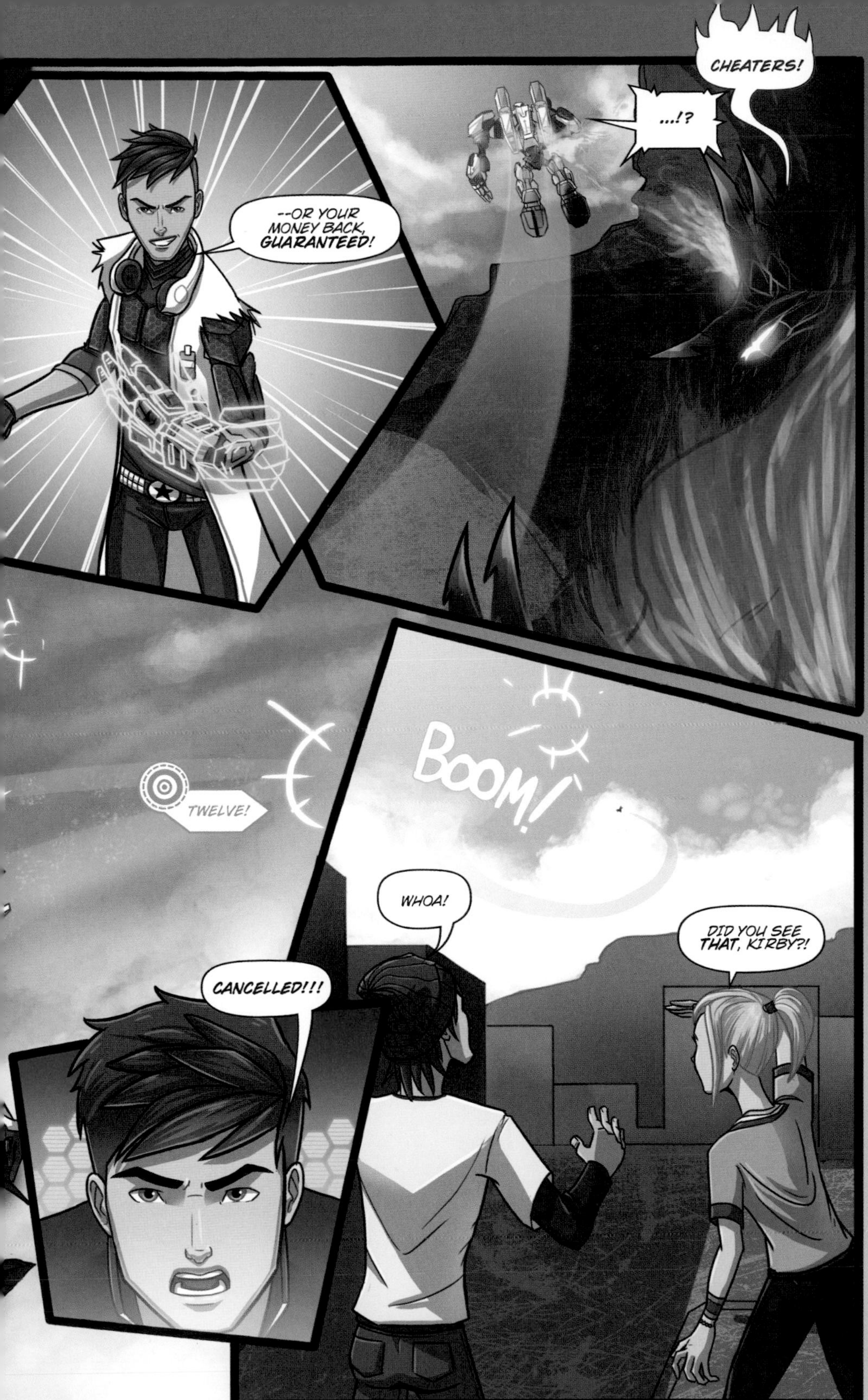
--OR YOUR MONEY BACK, GUARANTEED!
CHEATERS!
...!?
TWELVE!
BOOM!
CANCELLED!!!
WHOA!
DID YOU SEE THAT, KIRBY?!

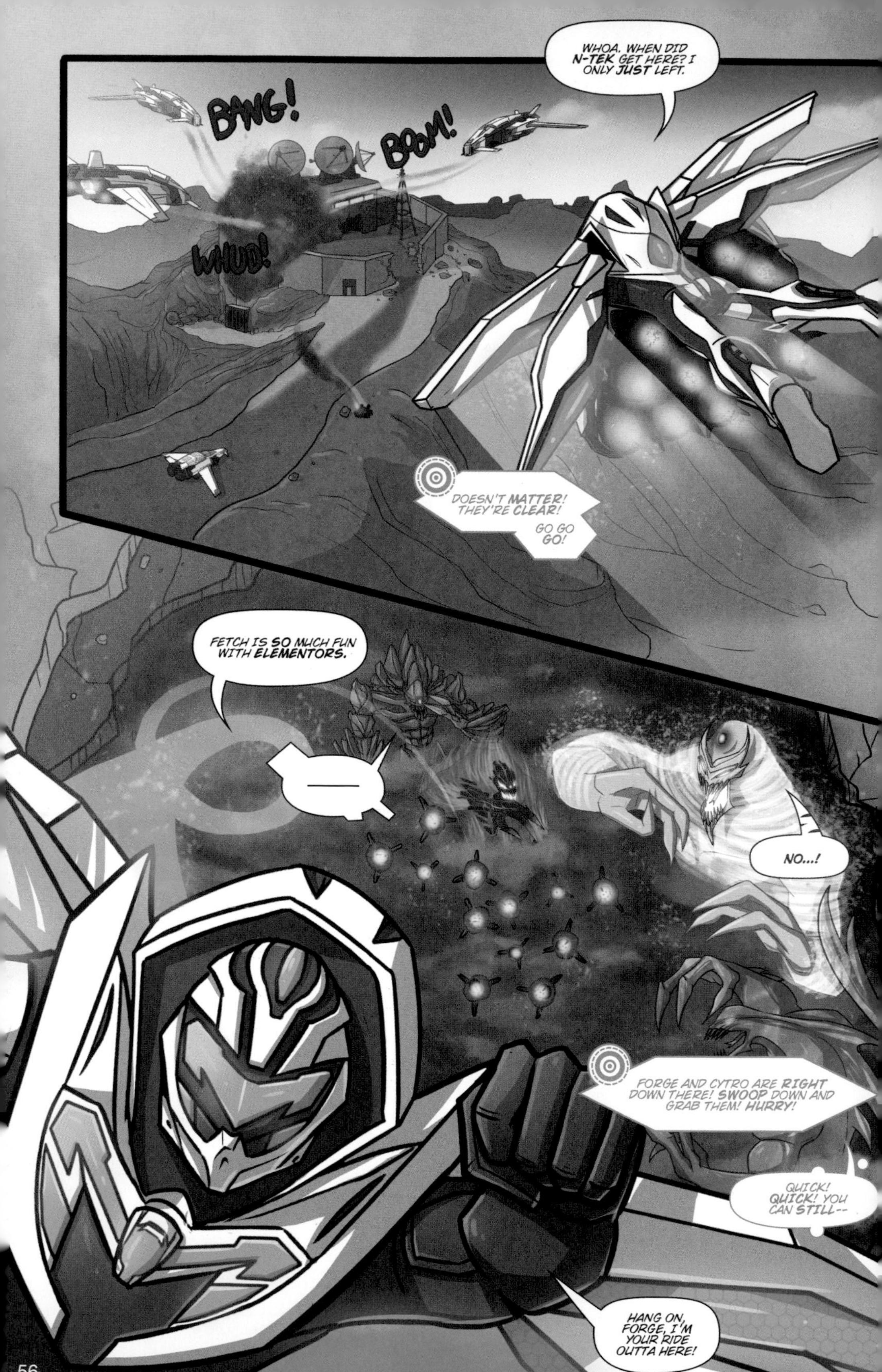
WHOA. WHEN DID N-TEK GET HERE? I ONLY JUST LEFT.
BANG!
BOOM!
WHUD!
DOESN'T MATTER! THEY'RE CLEAR!
GO GO GO!
FETCH IS SO MUCH FUN WITH ELEMENTORS.
NO...!
FORGE AND CYTRO ARE RIGHT DOWN THERE! SWOOP DOWN AND GRAB THEM! HURRY!
QUICK! QUICK! YOU CAN STILL--
HANG ON, FORGE, I'M YOUR RIDE OUTTA HERE!

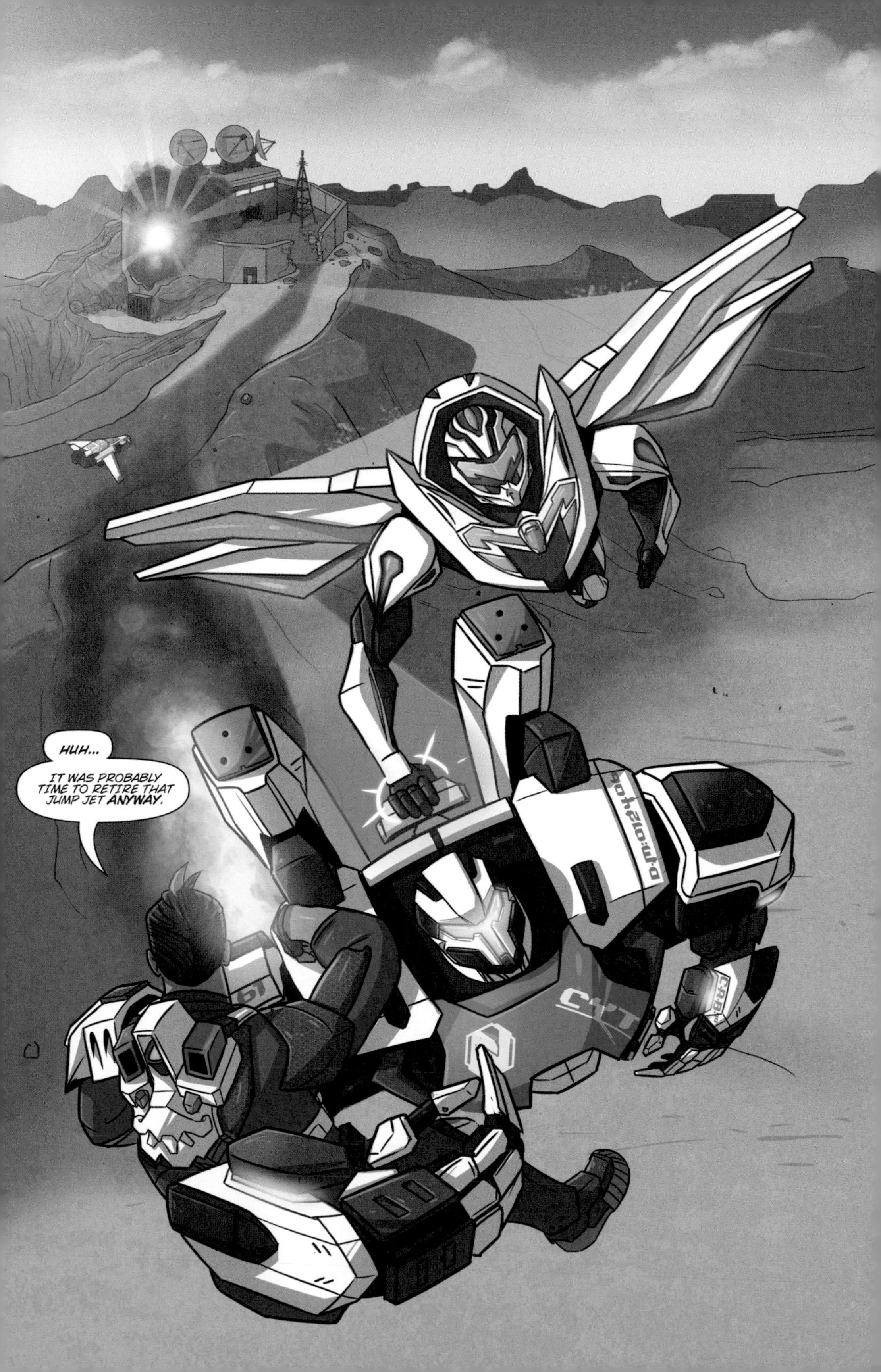
HUH...
IT WAS PROBABLY TIME TO RETIRE THAT JUMP JET ANYWAY.

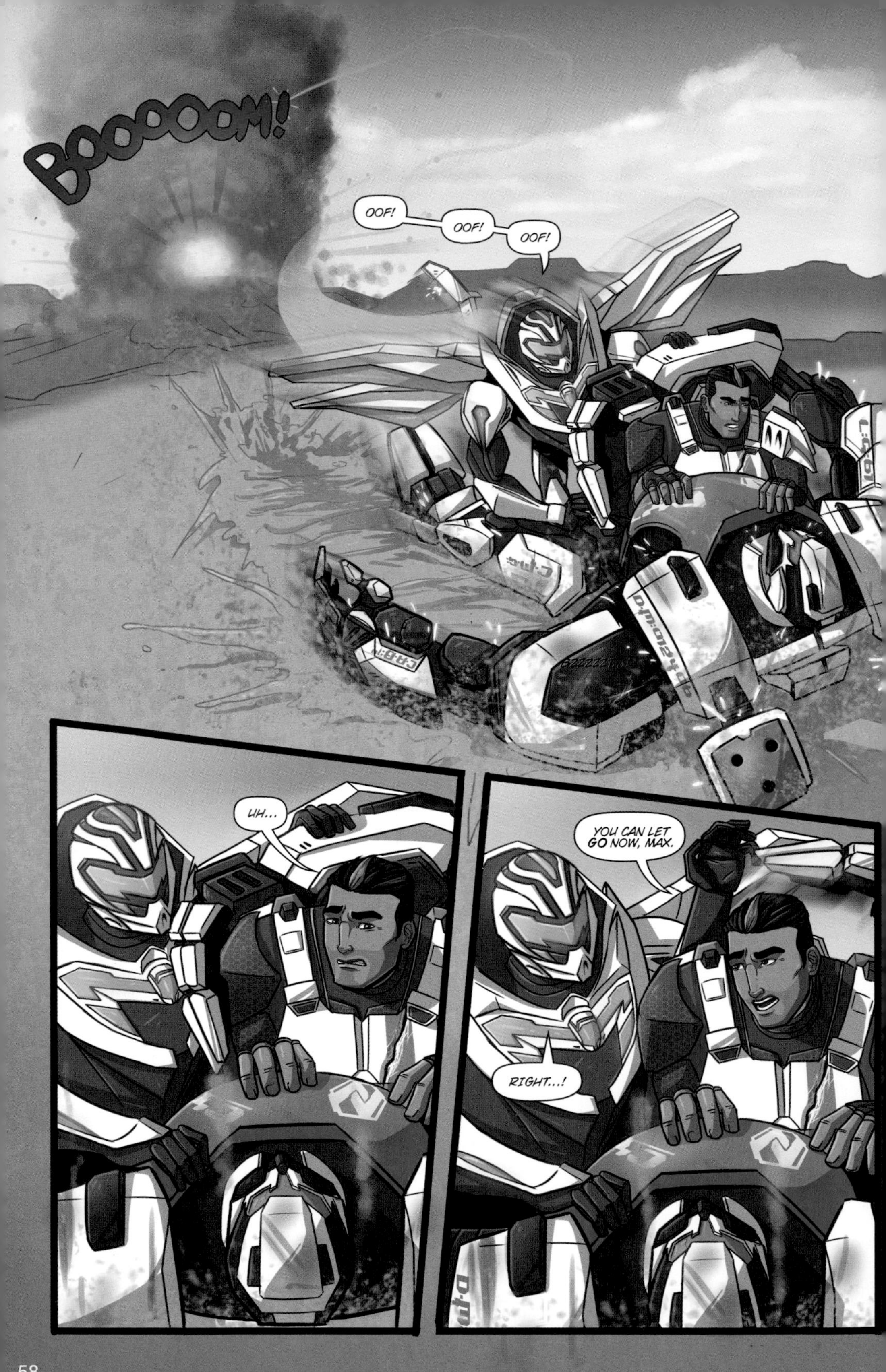
BOOOOOM!
OOF!
OOF!
OOF!
UH...
YOU CAN LET GO NOW, MAX.
RIGHT...!

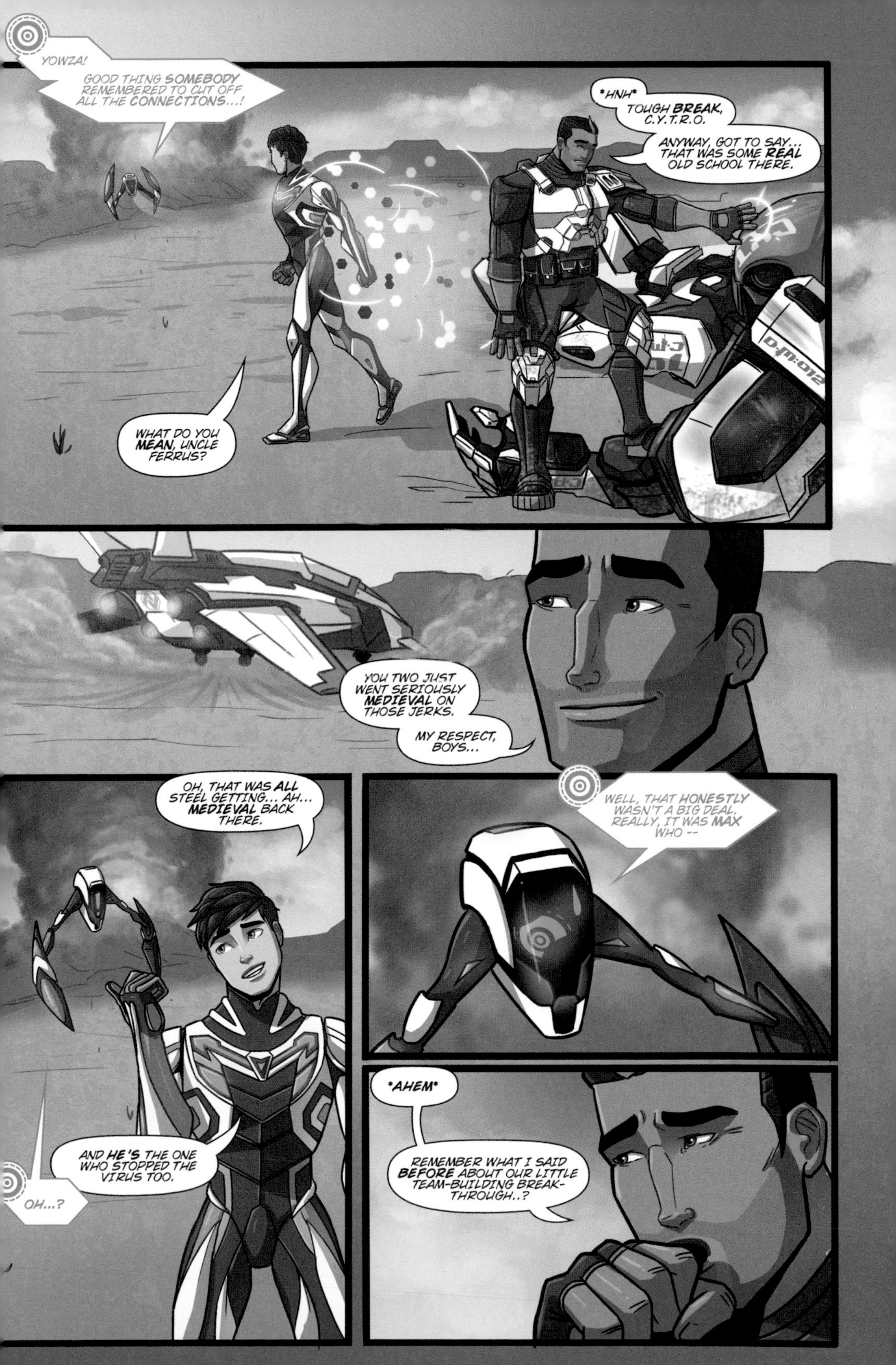
YOWZA!
GOOD THING SOMEBODY REMEMBERED TO CUT OFF ALL THE CONNECTIONS...!
HNH TOUGH BREAK, C.Y.T.R.O.
ANYWAY, GOT TO SAY... THAT WAS SOME REAL OLD SCHOOL THERE.
WHAT DO YOU MEAN, UNCLE FERRUS?
YOU TWO JUST WENT SERIOUSLY MEDIEVAL ON THOSE JERKS.
MY RESPECT, BOYS...
OH, THAT WAS ALL STEEL GETTING... AH... MEDIEVAL BACK THERE.
WELL, THAT HONESTLY WASN'T A BIG DEAL. REALLY, IT WAS MAX WHO --
AND HE'S THE ONE WHO STOPPED THE VIRUS TOO.
OH...?
AHEM
REMEMBER WHAT I SAID BEFORE ABOUT OUR LITTLE TEAM-BUILDING BREAK-THROUGH..?

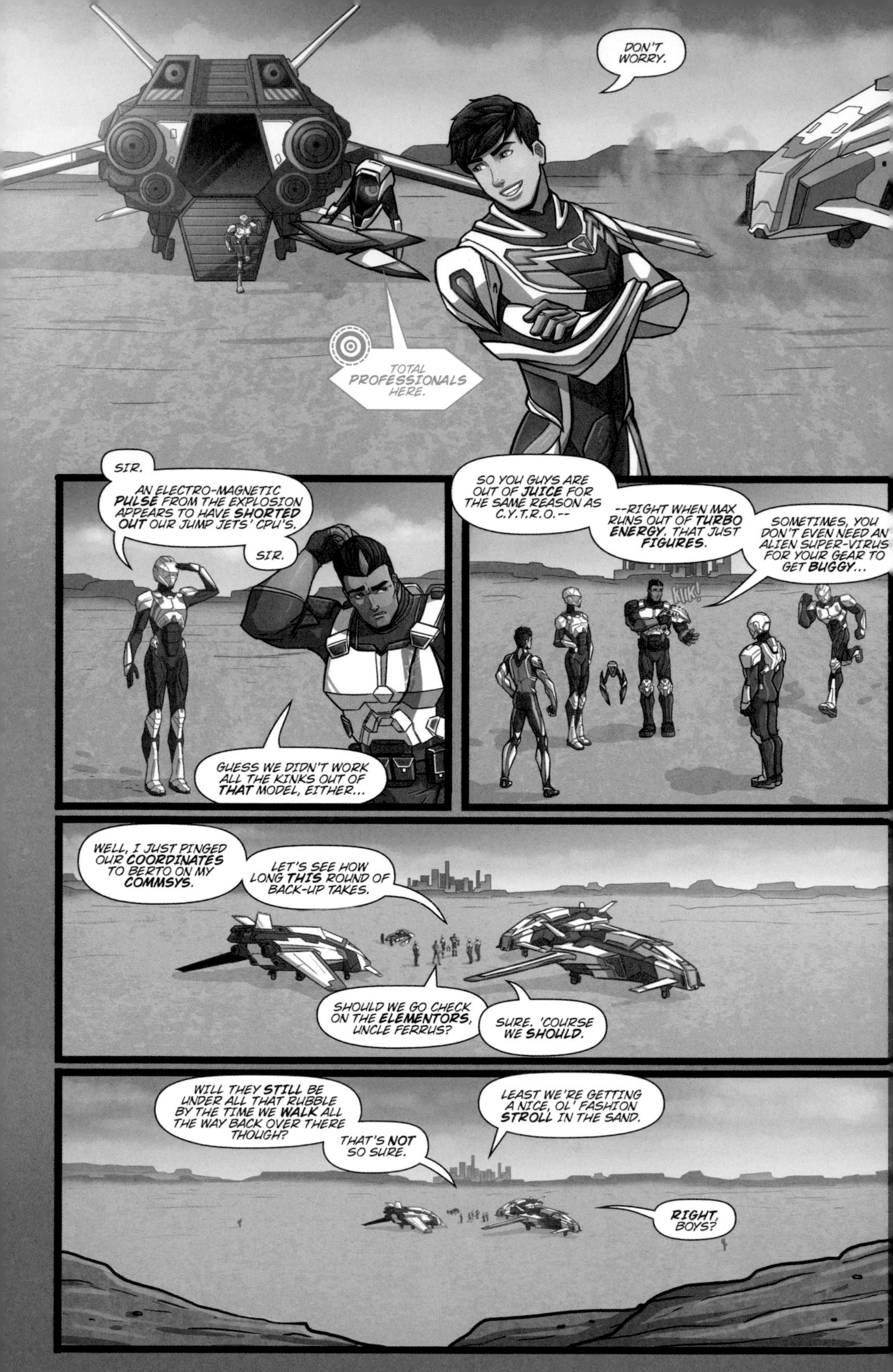

DON'T WORRY.
TOTAL PROFESSIONALS HERE.
SIR.
AN ELECTRO-MAGNETIC PULSE FROM THE EXPLOSION APPEARS TO HAVE SHORTED OUT OUR JUMP JETS' CPU'S.
SIR.
GUESS WE DIDN'T WORK ALL THE KINKS OUT OF THAT MODEL, EITHER...
SO YOU GUYS ARE OUT OF JUICE FOR THE SAME REASON AS C.Y.T.R.O.--
--RIGHT WHEN MAX RUNS OUT OF TURBO ENERGY. THAT JUST FIGURES.
SOMETIMES, YOU DON'T EVEN NEED AN ALIEN SUPER-VIRUS FOR YOUR GEAR TO GET BUGGY...
KLIK!
WELL, I JUST PINGED OUR COORDINATES TO BERTO ON MY COMMSYS.
LET'S SEE HOW LONG THIS ROUND OF BACK-UP TAKES.
SHOULD WE GO CHECK ON THE ELEMENTORS, UNCLE FERRUS?
SURE. 'COURSE WE SHOULD.
WILL THEY STILL BE UNDER ALL THAT RUBBLE BY THE TIME WE WALK ALL THE WAY BACK OVER THERE THOUGH?
THAT'S NOT SO SURE.
LEAST WE'RE GETTING A NICE, OL' FASHION STROLL IN THE SAND.
RIGHT, BOYS?

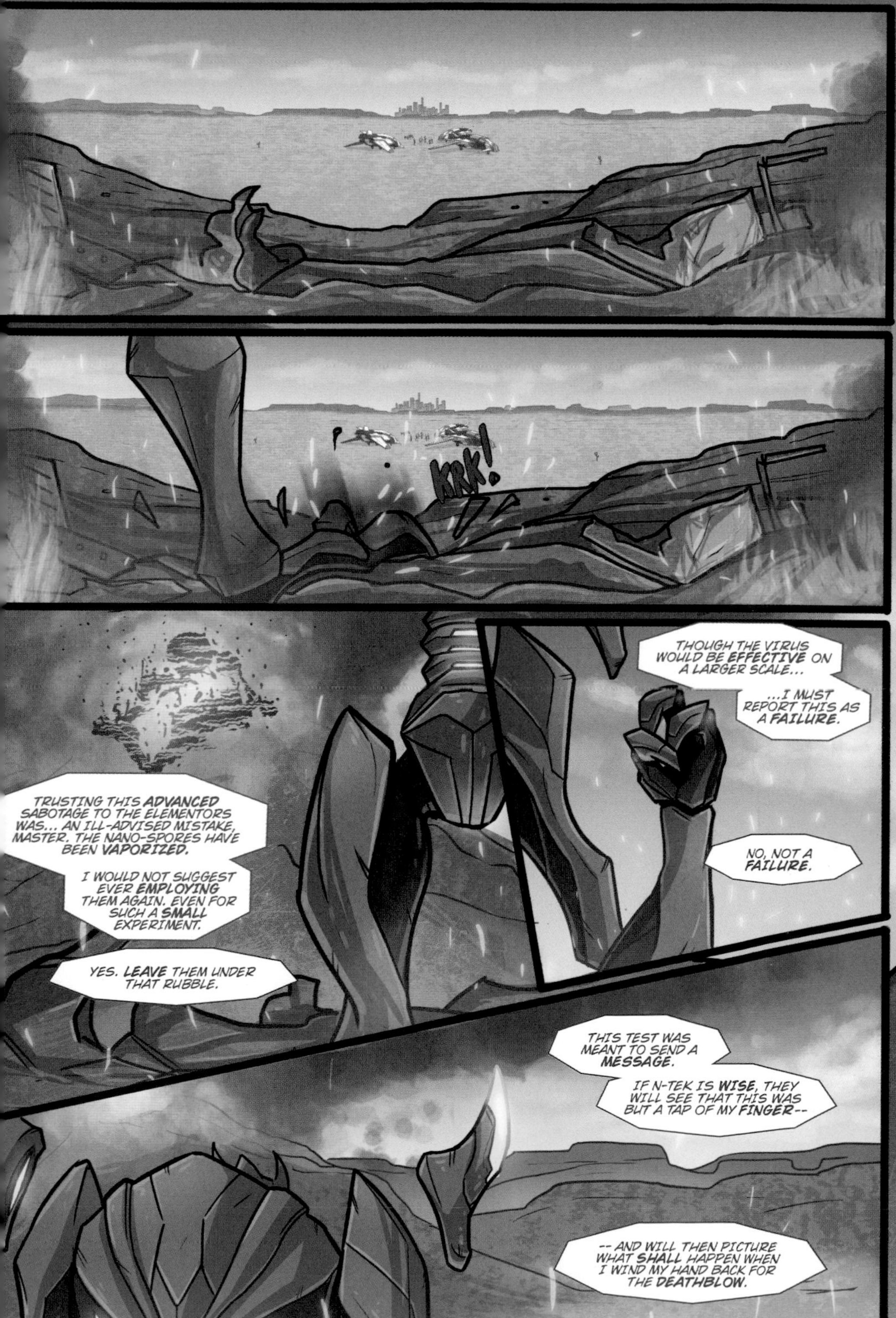
KRK!
THOUGH THE VIRUS WOULD BE EFFECTIVE ON A LARGER SCALE...
...I MUST REPORT THIS AS A FAILURE.
TRUSTING THIS ADVANCED SABOTAGE TO THE ELEMENTORS WAS... AN ILL-ADVISED MISTAKE, MASTER. THE NANO-SPORES HAVE BEEN VAPORIZED.
I WOULD NOT SUGGEST EVER EMPLOYING THEM AGAIN. EVEN FOR SUCH A SMALL EXPERIMENT.
NO, NOT A FAILURE.
YES. LEAVE THEM UNDER THAT RUBBLE.
THIS TEST WAS MEANT TO SEND A MESSAGE.
IF N-TEK IS WISE, THEY WILL SEE THAT THIS WAS BUT A TAP OF MY FINGER--
--AND WILL THEN PICTURE WHAT SHALL HAPPEN WHEN I WIND MY HAND BACK FOR THE DEATHBLOW.

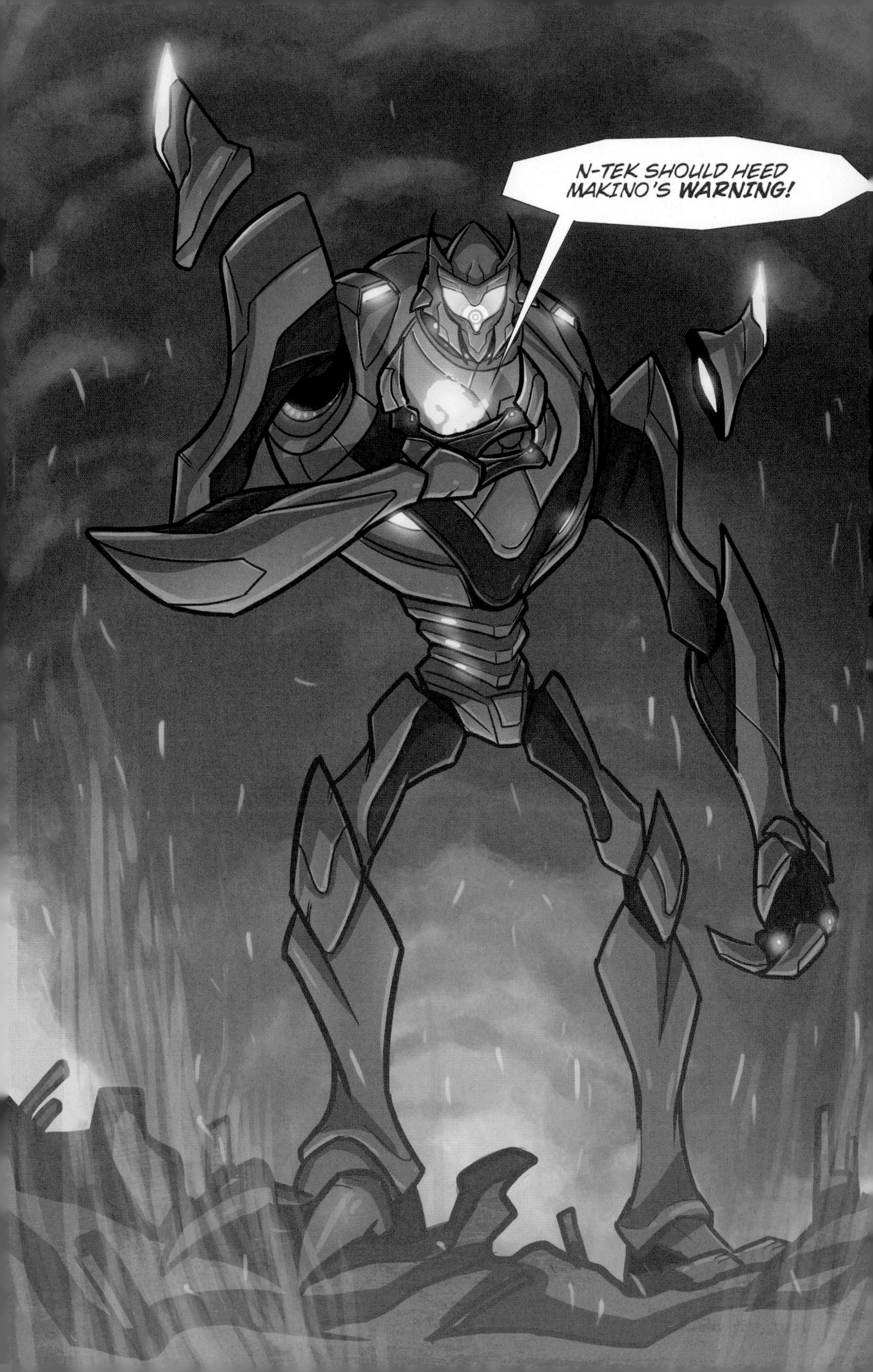
N-TEK SHOULD HEED MAKINO'S WARNING!

MAX STEEL™

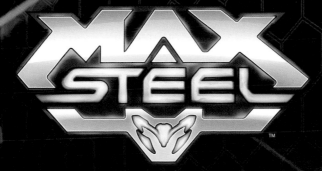

MAX STEEL™
Volume 3
Haywire

Story by Tom Pinchuk
Cover Art by Alfa Robbi
Cover Colors by Anang Setyawan
Interior Art by Jan Wijngaard
Letters by Zack Turner

Design/Sam Elzway
Editor/Joel Enos

Special thanks to Gabriel DeLaTorre, Lloyd Goldfine, Cindy Ledermann, Michael Montalvo, Jocelyn Morgan, Julia Phelps and Darren Sander.

Printed in China

Published by VIZ Media, LLC
P.O. Box 77010
San Francisco, CA 94107

10 9 8 7 6 5 4 3 2 1
First printing, April 2014

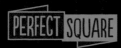

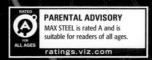

PERFECT SQUARE

RATED A FOR ALL AGES
PARENTAL ADVISORY
MAX STEEL is rated A and is suitable for readers of all ages.
ratings.viz.com

viz media
www.viz.com

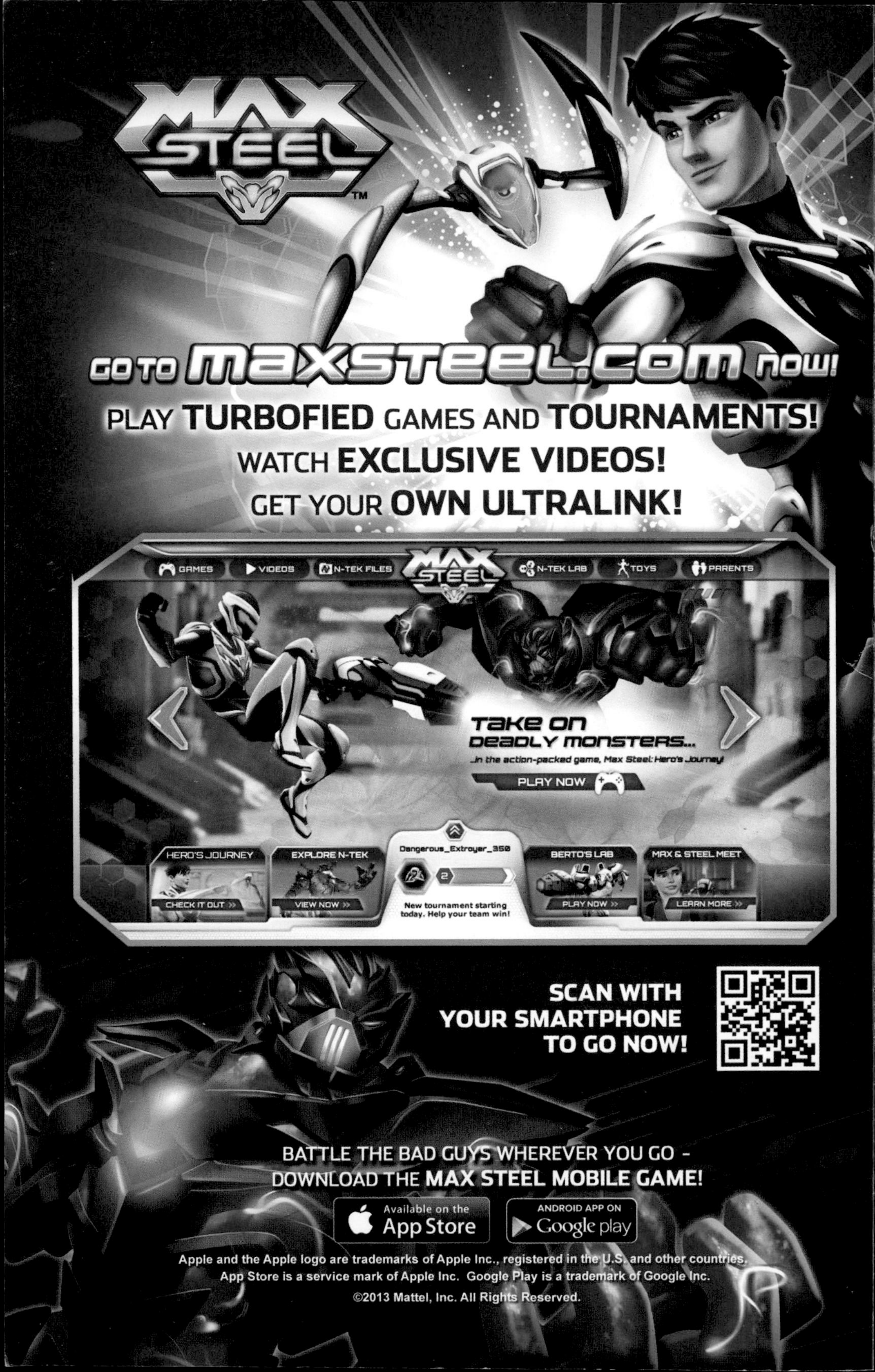
MAX STEEL™
GO TO MAXSTEEL.COM NOW!
PLAY TURBOFIED GAMES AND TOURNAMENTS!
WATCH EXCLUSIVE VIDEOS!
GET YOUR OWN ULTRALINK!
GAMES
VIDEOS
N-TEK FILES
MAX STEEL
N-TEK LAB
TOYS
PARENTS
TAKE ON DEADLY MONSTERS...
...in the action-packed game, Max Steel: Hero's Journey!
PLAY NOW
HERO'S JOURNEY
CHECK IT OUT »
EXPLORE N-TEK
VIEW NOW »
Dangerous_Extroyer_350
New tournament starting today. Help your team win!
BERTO'S LAB
PLAY NOW »
MAX & STEEL MEET
LEARN MORE »
SCAN WITH YOUR SMARTPHONE TO GO NOW!
BATTLE THE BAD GUYS WHEREVER YOU GO -
DOWNLOAD THE MAX STEEL MOBILE GAME!
Available on the App Store
ANDROID APP ON Google play
Apple and the Apple logo are trademarks of Apple Inc., registered in the U.S. and other countries.
App Store is a service mark of Apple Inc. Google Play is a trademark of Google Inc.
©2013 Mattel, Inc. All Rights Reserved.